A STRANGER'S KISS

LORDS OF CHANCE BOOK ONE

TARAH SCOTT

CHAPTER 1

THE GARDEN PARTY

OLIVIA SLAMMED HER GLASS OF LEMONADE DOWN ON THE TABLE. The *cad*. Had he no shame? He was *her* fiancé—or would be soon. Yet there he was, Timothy Menzies, pulling Maggie Wilkins behind the hawthorn hedgerow in Lady Blair's garden.

"Olivia, darling, do you have any more *Summertime Melody* books? The one with the new arrangement of *Robin Adair*?" Lady Kendrick called out as Olivia stormed past the summer tent spread out on the lawn.

"Louisa sang so wonderfully this afternoon," another voice chimed amidst choruses of agreement.

Then, of course, the inevitable murmurings, all a variation of, "Isn't that the Mad Printer's daughter?"

Olivia rolled her eyes and continued on as if she hadn't heard. Right now, she was keen on giving the two-timing Timothy Menzies a piece of her mind. Questions of song and everything else could wait.

With a scowl, she marched around the hedgerow. She was

treated to an impressive view of Lady Blair's stately Wedder-burn Manor, a majestic backdrop to the formal garden that sprawled before her in a fine array of climbing roses, lilacs, and sculpted boxwoods.

At first, she couldn't spot him, but the shaking limbs of a boxwood to the left drew her attention. Timothy. Not more than a dozen yards away behind a marble Italian bust. He stood with an awkward arm locked around Maggie's waist and his lips attached to hers like a leech. Olivia huffed. Just what did Maggie have that she didn't? They were practically twins—both redheads with bright green eyes and voluptuous curves.

As if sensing her eyes burning holes through his head, Timothy turned and squinted in her direction. He froze.

Olivia's nostrils flared.

He cringed, looking as guilty as sin.

She couldn't lose him—not that she loved him, of course—but now with her father disabled, she needed a husband. Desperately. Her father's music shop stood on the brink of ruin and now that the bankers understood he'd never recover, they had given Olivia an ultimatum: sell the shop or hand it over to a husband, as a proper woman should.

Unfortunately, finding a husband had proved a daunting challenge. Timothy, as the fourth son of a bookbinder, had been her best possibility, by far. He could scarcely do better than to marry her. She could tolerate him—barely.

Yet, as she saw him with his arm hooked around Maggie's waist—of all women, *why her?* —a sense of anger warred with hurt pride.

The anger won. With a scowl, Olivia planted her hands on her hips. Her left elbow struck something that gave way only slightly. A harsh intake of breath behind her made her realize she'd just elbowed the gut of a passing stranger.

"Pardon me," she tossed a distracted apology over her shoulder.

"My pleasure, I assure you," a man's deep baritone rumbled above her left ear, much higher than she usually heard.

He had to be tall. Timothy was short and incredibly sensitive over the matter. Without a second thought, Olivia whirled, grabbed the stranger by his neckcloth, rose on her tiptoes and planted a kiss over his startled lips. He was even taller than she expected. She would have missed his mouth entirely and kissed his chin instead had he not obligingly dipped the last inch or two.

The pleasing blend of soap and sandalwood eddied around her. The man's lips unexpectedly parted beneath hers. Surprised, Olivia dropped to her heels. His head dipped with her, never breaking contact as his tongue teased the seam of her lips. Instinct opened her mouth. His tongue immediately slid over hers, the soft warmth along with the roughness of his chin sending a frisson of awareness straight down to her toes.

Olivia's lashes flew open. Just when had she closed them? Was this even a kiss? She'd never experienced shivers in other parts of her body when Timothy had dropped a peck on her mouth.

She wrenched free of the man and stepped back. She caught only the briefest impression of blond hair, laughing gray eyes, and a strong, dimpled chin before he'd caught her about the waist and swung her back into the circle of his arms.

"Have a care, lass." His chest vibrated against her breasts.

He stepped back, pulling her with him as a footman barreled around the hedgerow behind them. The footman gasped and lifted his tray of lemon ices over Olivia's head. He danced sideways. The crystal glasses clinked and wobbled precariously as he attempted to regain his balance.

He succeeded. Barely. Drawing a deep breath, he schooled his features and politely dipped his chin. "Pardon me, my lord, miss."

"Bravo, well done," the man holding Olivia commended with a chuckle.

With a formal nod, the footman spun smartly on his heel and hurried off toward the tent. The hard muscles beneath Olivia shifted. She held still, acutely aware of a hard abdomen, long thighs, and the arm so casually looped around her waist. Her heart skipped a beat as every nerve in her body flared to life. She'd never known such intimate contact with a man could have such a heightening effect. The experience was far different than she'd imagined.

"It has been a pleasure, Miss," the man began.

Embarrassed, she twisted free of his embrace, and then suddenly remembered Timothy. A quick glance toward the hedgerow revealed both Timothy and his redheaded lover had gone.

"I daresay, you succeeded in making the sallow-faced fop jealous," the man behind her commented in a knowing voice.

Fop? Olivia winced. The description fit Timothy more than she cared to admit. Still, she tossed her head and lifted her chin. "I wait for no one. I was merely illustrating that fact. He's no longer welcome to keep my company, good sir."

She faced the man and, for the first time, noticed the fine quality of his immaculate white shirt, gray silk cravat, and double-breasted, velvet-trimmed waistcoat. Expensive and of the highest quality. The clothes of a nobleman.

Wincing, she hastily amended, "Eh...my lord."

Again, he chuckled. The sound drew her eyes from his midriff to his face. Sweet Lord above, the man was handsome. He towered over her, his gray eyes glinting with amusement over his strong, straight nose. Then, her gaze dropped to his lips. They appeared as sensual as they'd felt. She shivered.

A light summer breeze blew through the garden, ruffling his blond hair as he peered down at her with brow cocked. "Only a fool would risk losing a lass like you." His lip quirked.

Olivia's eyes widened.

"A real man doesn't let the lass that caught his interest slip through his fingers. He goes after her." His lips widened into a mischievous grin, then he lowered his voice to add, "Rather like this."

Before she could respond, he caught her close. His fingers splayed low over the base of her spine as he molded her body against his. A wave of liquid heat flooded straight to her core as his tongue immediately sought entry to her mouth. She didn't hesitate. She opened her lips, breathing him in as he swept inside. For a timeless moment, their tongues tangled. Warm. Wet. She dug her fingers into his waistcoat to steady herself. He moaned, a soft sound, more intimate than she'd ever heard, and then, slowly, he pulled away.

His laugh was a lazy one, full of satisfaction. "A true man kisses the woman he's interested in—precisely like that."

He stepped away, executed a gallant bow, swung on his heel, and strode through the garden toward the gray stone manor without a backward glance. Dazed, Olivia watched him go, unable to tear her gaze from his narrow hips and the line of his broad shoulders. Lord help her, but after him, how could she ever make peace with Timothy's fumbling pecks and awkward, one-armed hugs? Who knew such kisses truly existed outside the pages of a book?

"Olivia?"

Startled, Olivia jerked as her friend, Louisa, joined her. Beautiful Louisa Hamilton, a well-endowed opera singer with a lark's voice and a body that drove men mad, knew how to use both of her assets to her advantage. She smiled at Olivia, every strand of her elaborately coifed, raven hair in place and each fold of her rose satin gown artfully arranged.

Olivia nodded a greeting and ignored the customary twinge of envy she felt in Louisa's presence. She'd never attain such elegance and beauty. She simply hadn't the time nor patience to primp for hours in front of the mirror, painstakingly painting her face, even to the darkening of each individual eyelash.

"Did you find him?" Louisa's brown eyes sparkled with anticipation.

Olivia frowned, puzzled. "Who?"

Louisa covered her mouth with her hands and giggled. "Your lips are swollen. He kissed you, didn't he? A real kiss this time. I *knew* he couldn't resist you in that green gown."

Olivia blinked and glanced down at the green-sprigged muslin she'd borrowed from Louisa just that morning.

"There's no need to be shy," Louisa chided. "Tell me, Olivia. Do. I didn't think Timothy knew *how* to kiss."

He obviously didn't—not if one could call what the nobleman had done a kiss. Olivia shook her head. The experience had been far too intense to share, especially with Louisa. Glasgow's gossips would be chattering about the Mad Printer's lusty daughter within the hour. Maybe even less.

"Oh, fiddlesticks." Louisa rolled her eyes and gave Olivia's arm a disappointed tug. Her face brightened. "Don't fret. I will pull each delicious detail from your lips at my house party."

Again, Olivia shook her head. "I really must return to the shop."

"Nonsense. You're coming," Louisa announced firmly. "I sang your songs, did I not?"

Olivia clenched her jaw. She'd hardly sung the songs for free. While they were friends, they weren't of the bosom buddy kind. She'd paid Louisa a fine penny to sing and she had the contracts safely tucked away under the print shop's floorboards as proof—but disagreeing with Louisa was always a losing proposition. The opera singer altered facts to suit her fancy.

Still, Olivia simply wasn't in the mood to attend a party—especially one of Louisa's raucous ones. "I cannot."

"They never rush to the print shop to buy the sheet music *this* quickly, silly," Louisa reproved in a teasing tone. "But even if they should, you still have your shop boy, don't you?"

"William?" Olivia grimaced. She struggled to keep shop boys. She'd hired William only a month ago and had already caught him asleep on the press room floor in the broad light of day nearly a dozen times. Still, as lazy as he was, he was the only one she could afford. "Yes, he's there," she muttered, then with a roll of her eyes, added, "And perhaps even awake."

Louisa snorted. "Just come for an hour or two, and then I will have my coachman take you home. No doubt, you'll arrive at the same time as if you'd walked."

That made Olivia smile. Her feet still ached from the morning's trip. She gave in with a sigh. "Very well."

"Then I will say my farewells as you jot down your music orders. Let's meet at my carriage, say, in half an hour?"

Olivia nodded and Louisa dashed away across the expanse of green lawn with a lightness in her step that indicated a man was involved. Olivia pursed her lips, a little jealous. Louisa never lacked for suitors, though none had, as yet, proposed marriage. Not that Timothy had, despite the number of times Olivia had prodded him.

She scowled, irritated to find herself hunting for a husband yet again. The bankers had agreed to meet her next week—wanting an introduction to her fiancé. Perhaps she'd pushed Timothy too fast…

She blew her hair out of her face, opened her reticule and fished out her pencil along with a sheet of paper. Time to work. The charity event had entered the tea-drinking stage, the time when the attendees relaxed with their cups of Pekoe and gossiped about the afternoon's performance behind their fans. Today, they would have little to critique. Louisa had delivered a fine performance. So fine, in fact, that Olivia wondered if she'd printed enough copies of *Robin Adair*.

Teacups clinked, and the scent of lilacs swirled around Olivia as she entered the tent.

"Olivia, darling, do tell me you have the version of *Robin Adair* that Miss Hamilton sang."

"I would so love a copy as well, my dear. Have your shop boy run the music over in the morning, will you?"

Olivia moved as quickly as she could through the tables, recording names and bobbing curtsies along the way. As she'd thought, requests for *Robin Adair* outnumbered all others, and this time, she heard the "Ah, the mad printer's daughter again, aye?" comments only twice. Not that such comments bothered her anymore. She was simply far too busy. She had a print shop to run, an infirm father to care for, and bills to pay.

When she finished her rounds, she tucked her paper and pencil back into her reticule and headed toward Lady Blair's table to bid her farewell. The Lady Blair of Wedderburn Manor sat at the tent's edge near the lilacs, relaxed in her latticework chair while chatting with Glasgow's premiere gossip, the Lady Kendrick. Though both women were of the same age, Lady Blair seemed far younger. Even though her face lacked wrinkles and her figure rivaled the season's slender debutantes, her perpetual youth stemmed more from the kindness of her heart than any physical attribute.

Lady Kendrick, on the other hand, though rail thin, twitched and fidgeted in a manner that reminded Olivia of a mouse. Today, dressed in a brown gown adorned with drooping gray feathers, Olivia couldn't help but think she resembled one.

As Lady Blair's distinct silvery laughter filtered through the tent, Olivia paused. How many times had she stood in this exact spot and listened to Lady Blair laugh with her very own dear mother, the disowned Lady Glenna of Lennox?

Of all her mother's friends, only Lady Blair had remained at her mother's side and helped her through the pain she'd endured from her family over daring to wed her true love—a poor music publisher's son with no title--instead of her family's choice of groom. Only Lady Blair had continued to invite her mother to Wedderburn Manor for tea, even after her father, the Duke of Lennox, disowned her and proclaimed his younger daughter, Arlene, his heir. He'd announced his decision during a lavish ball and publicly bestowed upon Arlene the famed Lennox Blue Slipper, as family tradition dictated.

"The Blue Slipper was to have been yours, Glenna." Lady Blair frowned as she poured the tea.

"Nonsense. I would have made a dismal Duchess." Olivia's mother had laughed, then smiled at Olivia where she played near the lilacs. "Anyway, what need have I for a sapphire slipper? I have the wealth of the world, right there, in a little sprite with ink-stained hands."

Lady Blair waved for Olivia to join them.

"She takes after her father, so very much. I swear she already knows how to operate the printing press better than he does...."

Olivia closed her eyes and drew a deep breath. She missed her mother. So much. The nearly four years since the carriage accident had been hard ones. She brushed the tears at the corners of her eyes, lifted her lashes and forced her feet forward.

"They say Lord Randall is desperate," Lady Kendrick said as Olivia arrived. "He must find a rich wife and soon, but with a temper as black as a chimney sweeper's feet...well, I wish him luck."

Lady Blair graciously dipped her head. "I knew him as a child. He grew up with my dear Nicholas."

"Well, what can I say?" Lady Kendrick lowered her voice, "They say Lord Randall's been keeping company with those opera singers—and *more* than one." The mousy woman's nose twitched as her lips quivered in a salacious smile.

Olivia lifted a brow. Lord help her, the only things the woman lacked were whiskers and a tail.

Lady Blair's face brightened as Olivia arrived. "Olivia, child. I've missed you so."

"Lady Blair, Lady Kendrick." Olivia curtsied deeply. She'd spent the past fifteen minutes bobbing up and down for the sake of a sale, but this time, she meant every inch of respect as she curtsied low before Lady Blair.

"Come now, Olivia," Lady Blair admonished as she grasped Olivia's forearm and lifted her upright. "You are the daughter of my dearest friend, and if I may say so, the daughter I wish I had."

Again, tears misted Olivia's lashes.

Lady Blair squeezed her arm in silent sympathy, and then let her go. "Unfortunately, you've just missed my dear Nicholas. He's off to Edinburgh, again. I would so love the two of you to meet."

Olivia smiled. Poor Lady Blair. Her son was well-known as a notorious rake. Not for the first time, she wondered how such a lovely woman could produce such a son. "Perhaps another time, my lady," she demurred.

"Yes, yes, my dear." Lady Blair sighed, then smiled. "Perhaps he can join us in Glasgow for your event. What was it called? Ah yes, *An Enchanted Summer Evening*. When will the tickets be sold?"

The question elicited a small rush of excitement. One more payment to the Theater Royale and then, finally, Glasgow would hear her father's music: *An Enchanted Summer Evening*, songs by Oliver Mackenzie. There would be no 'Mad Printer' comments after that. Glasgow would stand in awe, and since she'd be the only publisher to print the music, she'd finally free the shop from debt.

"Soon, my lady," Olivia promised.

"Pray tell, you are not encouraging this foolish venture, Lady Blair?" a testy voice rasped from behind.

Lady Blair rose swiftly to her feet. "Your Grace," she murmured, her eyes locked over Olivia's shoulder.

Olivia turned as a craggy-faced man with salt-and-pepper hair joined them, tall and distinguished in his green plaid kilt. Judging from his black brows drawn into a scowl and the way his jaw jutted, he was greatly displeased. Olivia dropped a quick curtsey and began backing away.

The man's eyes narrowed into slits. "Olivia," he grated, his lips barely opening as if speaking through clenched teeth.

Olivia blinked. He knew her name? She'd never met him in her life. He was obviously wealthy, a noble of repute. The smallest of the rings glittered on his knobby fingers in testament to his wealth. Never had she seen so large a sapphire. No doubt, he mistook her for someone else.

"My lord." She inched away.

"Olivia," he said, again.

Bobbing again, Olivia cast a puzzled glance at Lady Blair for guidance, but to her shock, Lady Blair appeared almost stricken. A meadowlark landed in the lilacs behind her, its chirp unnaturally loud in the silence that had fallen over the tent.

"Olivia," the stern man repeated.

Olivia faced the man again. His eyes, so very green and so very cold, narrowed as she frowned. "My lord?"

When he didn't answer, Lady Blair cleared her throat. "My dear Olivia, may I introduce His Grace, the Duke of Lennox."

Lennox. Olivia stared into the man's eyes for a full five seconds before recognition struck.

Lennox. *The* Duke of Lennox.

Lord save her.

He was her grandfather.

CHAPTER 2

"Olivia," the impressive Duke of Lennox repeated her name for the fourth time, slowly, as if acquainting his tongue with a foreign word.

Olivia couldn't move. As a child, she'd imagined her grandfather as a cruel, hawk-nosed man with a presence so overpoweringly evil that even the woodland animals scattered before him in fear of their lives. Now that she stood in his presence, she realized she'd erred. Her younger self had forgotten to account for the chill of his eyes.

"Olivia." This time, the name slipped from his lips a bit easier.

She drew a steadying breath. What was she to say? This man had broken her mother's heart. He'd refused to acknowledge his own daughter even in death. He hadn't even written a letter of condolence. What did he expect from her? That she would trip over her feet to curtsey just because he'd finally learned to pronounce her name? Nae, she'd never bend her knees to him—never again. Olivia lifted her chin and eyed him warily. Something gleamed in the green eyes locked with hers —a spark of anger? She didn't care.

The duke's head swiveled to the side. "Deborah," he barked.

The voices in the tent buzzed, soft and low, as a young, rosy-cheeked brunette popped up from a nearby table and rushed to join them.

"Deborah, this is Olivia." The duke's chilling eyes latched onto Olivia's once more. "Olivia is leaving. Now. Go with her."

Fortunately for him, she didn't want to stay a moment longer in his company. With the barest dip of her chin, Olivia spun on her heel, keenly aware of the gasps spreading through the tent. No doubt, by morning, even London would know how the duke's disowned granddaughter had publicly snubbed him—courtesy of Lady Kendrick. No doubt, the woman maintained a secret flock of carrier pigeons at her command.

Olivia marched through the tent and out into the lawn. She was halfway to the manor house when she noticed a timid tug to her sleeve. She stopped and whirled.

The rosy-cheeked Deborah stood there, twisting her fingers nervously. "It's…it's a pleasure to finally meet you, Cousin Olivia." She gulped.

Olivia stared, still stunned at the sudden turn of events. Deborah winced, then bit her bottom lip and waited with downcast eyes. She was obviously a shy, nervous thing, but then, living under the shadow of a man such as their grandfather, how could she be anything else? Sympathy surged through Olivia, along with a sense of awkwardness. Just what did one say to long lost cousins?

"So, your mother is Arlene?" Olivia winced. Of course, her mother was Arlene. Her own mother had had only one sister.

Deborah laughed nervously, then looked away. "Mother passed away last year…in New York."

"New York?" Olivia blurted. Then, belatedly held out her hands in sympathy. "I am sorry, so sorry, Deborah."

Deborah shrugged but gripped Olivia's fingers tightly with her own. "Yes, New York. Grandfather disowned her several years ago," she answered with a nervous giggle that clearly held back an onslaught of tears.

Disowned? Olivia snorted in disbelief. Just how hateful *was* the old man? And why hadn't she heard a hint of the matter—not even from the source of all gossip, Lady Kendrick?

"She…well, Grandfather was furious over the gambling debts… Oh, please, can we not speak of something else?" Deborah squeezed Olivia's fingers tighter. "I cannot tell you how grateful I am to finally meet you, after all these years."

The sadness in her cousin's eyes pulled at Olivia's heart even as she marveled at the similarities in their lives. Deborah had lost her mother—a disowned one, no less—and her father, as well. According to Lady Kendrick, the man had died from scarlet fever when Arlene was a child.

Olivia gave her cousin a warm smile and clasped her hands in turn. "I am delighted to meet you, as well, I assure you." With the initial shock waning, her throat threatened to close at the mere thought of another family member—at last.

"Do come visit me, will you?" Deborah asked eagerly. "Tomorrow? I am staying at Grandfather's townhouse on Kintail Strand, near the river."

Olivia hesitated. She had type to set, ink to make, and the Devil's Tail on the press needed mending, but at her cousin's crestfallen look, she heard herself ask, "Teatime?"

For the first time, Deborah's smile lit her eyes. "Until tomorrow, then."

"Tomorrow," Olivia promised.

With a last nervous bob, Deborah scurried away. Olivia watched her go, still somewhat dazed. After a moment, she collected her thoughts and hurried to the carriage drive. She had work to do. It was time to deal with Louisa. Cousins and cold-hearted grandfathers would have to wait.

Olivia arrived at Louisa's carriage only to be told by the coachman that she'd already left Wedderburn Manor in the company of Lord Randall. She lifted a brow at memory of Lady Kendrick's chimney sweep comment. Perhaps, Louisa didn't know of the man's black temper?

"She left the carriage at your disposal, Miss," the coachman said, and hopped down to hand her in. "Where to?"

Olivia suppressed a sigh. She was sore tempted to return straight home, but such an act was a poor way to repay Louisa's generosity. Besides, she couldn't afford to offend the woman— not when she relied on her so heavily to sing her father's songs.

"Louisa's townhouse, please," she forced out.

With a sigh, she settled onto the leather seat. This visit would have to be a short one, bordering on scandalous. Olivia quirked her lip. If anyone, Louisa shouldn't mind; she and scandal lived hand-in-hand.

The late afternoon sun slanted over Glasgow's rooftops as the carriage rolled up to Louisa's townhouse. Olivia dashed through the carriage door and up the narrow walkway before the horses had barely clopped to a stop.

The dour maid greeted her with a surly nod. "Miss Louisa is in the drawing room, Miss." She nodded over her shoulder. "That way. Last door on the left."

Tugging the fingers of her gloves, Olivia guided herself down the narrow hall.

Muffled laughter penetrated the closed drawing room door. Olivia discerned at least a dozen voices—maybe more. She hesitated with a hand on the doorknob. Would Louisa even notice her absence? She'd half turned away when the door suddenly opened.

She couldn't see who opened the door. They vanished behind it in a rustle of silk. The room was dark. Louisa had drawn the thick brocade drapes over the windows, blocking nearly all light from the room. Only a thin line of grey sunlight filtered through at the very top. Then, her eyesight adjusted to the dim light.

She'd never been to a bordello, but she couldn't imagine it would look much different than the scandalous scene before her. Shamefully dressed women lounged next to high ranking society men on overstuffed couches, men Olivia often saw in Glasgow Green, strolling with their wives and children. Their wives would be furious to see them now, sprawled at these women's sides, nuzzling their necks or kissing them outright. Several had their hands down the front of the women's gowns, fondling their breasts.

Olivia pursed her lips. She'd obviously erred in accepting Louisa's offer. The sooner she left, the better. She stepped back when the brocade drapes shifted, enough to let a shaft of sunlight slip through.

She saw the woman's face first, or the bottom half, anyway. Her lips parted to accept a spoonful of something from a crystal glass, a lemon ice, perhaps. The man leaned forward and dragged the spoon over the woman's lip in a way that made Olivia exceedingly uncomfortable. Then the man's face entered the beam of light.

Olivia drew back, shocked. It was Mr. Pitt, owner of the Theatre Royale. Lord save her, she was as good as ruined if the man saw her here. She turned and fled down the hall. She nearly collided with Louisa as she rounded the corner.

"Heavens, what happened?" Louisa gasped.

"Mr. Pitt," Olivia hissed, rattled. "Louisa, you *know* he can't see me here."

"Oh, don't be such a nitwit." Louisa rolled her eyes and gave a tsk of disapproval. She'd changed into a shockingly lowcut, pink silk gown and had loosened her hair, so that the locks fell in curls over her bare shoulders. "Surely, you know there's only one thing keeping you from that loan?"

Olivia scowled. "Must you bring up Timothy now?" She'd been so distracted by her cousin that she'd scarcely remembered Timothy in the garden—or, for that matter, the mysterious stranger.

"Timothy?" Louisa's eyes widened with surprise. "Are you truly that dense?"

Olivia's scowl deepened. Whatever was the woman going on about? A husband was the only thing that prevented the banker from releasing her much-needed funds.

Louisa arched a perfectly plucked brow, then she grabbed Olivia by the arm and stepped forward, as if to pull her back to the drawing room.

Olivia twisted free from her grasp. "I would much rather go home, Louisa. It is high time I checked on father. He gets upset if I am gone too long."

Louisa planted her hands on her ample hips. "Mrs. Lambert is watching him, is she not?"

"Of course, but I cannot afford to pay her the entire day."

Louisa pointed down the hall at the drawing room door. "If you trotted down the hall and let Mr. Pitt have his way with you, you'd have *more* than enough to pay Mrs. Lambert every day of the week."

"Pardon?"

"Oh, do not play the fool, Olivia." Louisa eyed her incredulously. "Come now, surely, you cannot say you didn't know?"

"Didn't know?" She hadn't, but she was certainly beginning to understand now.

"Mr. Pitt has a particular taste for curves. It's clear he's hankering after yours. Let the man fondle a little. You might even enjoy yourself. Just close your eyes and pretend he's someone else—Timothy, if that is who you want."

Twice affronted, Olivia narrowed her eyes. "I have no interest in becoming a toy. I am doing a fine enough job of taking care of myself. Thank you."

"Truly?" Louisa smirked. "Have Glasgow's theaters,

assembly halls, and publishers agreed to promote your spon-
sorships, then?"

Olivia averted her gaze.

"As I thought," Louisa gloated and then leaned close. "Find a
sponsor of your own, Olivia. Give up the shop. Publishing
music belongs in the world of men."

The world of men? Olivia clenched her jaw and shot her a
rebellious scowl.

Before Louisa could reply, the dour-faced maid stepped
into view. "You have a visitor, ma'am."

Louisa turned to leave.

"Wait." Olivia caught her arm. "I want to go home. If you
could just call your carriage now?"

"Fine," the opera singer huffed, "but you're making a
mistake. Soon, you will have to swallow your pride." With a lift
of her chin, she hissed, "Just like the rest of us."

Not bloody likely. She'd live on the streets and beg before
she let a man like Mr. Pitt touch so much as a toe, but she knew
better than to object and alienate Louisa further.

"Louisa?" a man's deep baritone called from the entryway.

With a wide smile, Louisa picked up her skirts and nearly
bowled Olivia over in her haste to greet the man. Olivia rolled
her eyes and stalked to the nearby sitting room to wait for the
carriage. She'd give the man twenty minutes before heading
home herself. The last rays of sunlight cast a warm glow over
the rose-painted walls. To her relief, the room was empty. She
crossed to the large, comfortable leather wingback chair and
leaned over the back to peer through the window at the darkening sky. Even if she left that precise moment, she still
wouldn't get home before nightfall.

She drummed her fingers on the leather. With the amount
of type left to set, she'd have to burn the oil lamps tonight. She
knew better than to hope the shop boy had already set the
pages. He was near useless, but, please God, surely, he'd kept

the windows shut? Twice in the last week alone, he'd opened the shutters, complaining of the heat, and the scholar's cat, Mr. Peppers, had slipped inside. The last time, he'd gotten into the ink and left a trail of pawprints on the music she'd set out to dry. She'd lost an entire day's work.

"Beautiful," a man's soft voice murmured.

Olivia whirled. A man towered in the gathering gloom behind her, halfway between herself and the door. Dressed in dark clothes, he easily merged with the shadows, but the silver handle of his dapper walking stick glinted in the stray rays of light. Odd. She hadn't heard him enter. Apparently taking her silence as an invitation, he joined her by the chair, moving with the silence and grace of a cat. Olivia shivered. She would have truly thought him a bodiless spirit until the pleasant scent of cedar and mint swirled about her.

The last remnants of the day's light played over the face of the man staring down at her. He was handsome, virile, with intense blue eyes and a smile that curled the corner of his lip that seemed more than a mite suggestive. No doubt, he thought her one of the drawing room women.

"Beautiful," he whispered this time. He trailed his gaze slowly over her body, then added, "The sunset, so beautiful."

"Then, should you not be looking out the window, my lord?" she asked in arched tones.

His brows lifted, surprised, but the interest in his eyes only deepened. "Pardon me. Allow me to introduce myself. I am Lord James Randall. You are?"

Lord Randall, the man with a temper blacker than a chimney sweep, and a man that apparently caught Louisa's fancy. If they weren't already lovers, no doubt, they would be soon.

Lord Randall leaned close, his eyes hooded. "And you?" he repeated, deepening his voice.

Olivia cleared her throat. "Olivia. Olivia Mackenzie."

He shifted and something about him changed. "Olivia Mackenzie," he said. His tone now took on a formal cast. "Granddaughter to the Duke of Lennox?"

It was Olivia's turn to be surprised. "How did you know?"

A look of amusement flashed over his face. "Glasgow society has spoken of no one else but you tonight, my dear."

Olivia frowned. Of course, with Lady Kendrick involved, no doubt everyone in London already knew, as well. "Then, I fear Glasgow society will find their evening a disappointment."

"Why would that be, Miss Mackenzie?"

Miss Mackenzie? He looked down at her with only respect now. His suggestive manner had vanished entirely.

"Olivia?" Louisa barged through the door. "I have been looking…" The words died on her lips as her gaze fell upon Lord Randall.

Olivia stepped back at once, lest Louisa misunderstand. "If you will excuse me," she murmured to Lord Randall, then turned toward the door. "I am ready, Louisa. Is the carriage here?"

"You can wait on the step," she replied.

The coolness of her tone couldn't be missed.

"Surely, you don't have to leave so quickly, Miss Mackenzie?" Lord Randall queried as he followed her into the hall.

"Yes, she does," Louisa answered in her stead. "She has an ill father to attend, my lord." Eyes locked with Olivia's, she rubbed her palm over Lord Randall's chest in a blatant statement of ownership.

"Yes, I must go," Olivia quickly agreed. "Good evening."

She'd be foolish to stay a moment longer, not with the way Louisa stood there, marking her territory like an angry cat.

"Good evening," Louisa replied with a firm nod. With a flutter or her lashes at Lord Randall, she cooed, "The card table is ready, my lord. Shall we?"

To Olivia's horror, Lord Randall shook Louisa free with an

irritated clench of his jaw and stepped forward.

"Allow me to see you to your carriage, Miss Mackenzie." He offered his arm.

"That isn't necessary, my lord," Olivia said. She didn't have to glance at Louisa to know she was furious. "If you will excuse me, I must be going."

She marched to the door, keenly aware of Louisa's venomous glare boring through the back of her head. The dour-faced maid stood by the open door.

"Thank you." Olivia nodded with a tight smile.

She'd scarcely set foot on the stoop before the door clicked shut behind her. She bit her bottom lip, worried. *An Enchanted Summer Evening's* concert was less than two months away. She couldn't risk upsetting Louisa, but she couldn't soothe ruffled feathers tonight—not with Lord Randall's wandering eye in the house.

As the coach rolled into view, Olivia heaved a sigh and stepped into the street.

Who knew befriending opera singers would prove so troublesome?

THE STRAINS OF THE PIANO REACHED OLIVIA'S EARS AS SHE stepped into the dimly lit music shop. She smiled and stood still, as her father's music swept her back to a happier time.

Almost four years had passed since the carriage accident, but her heart still ached, almost as much as it had on the day of the tragedy itself. She'd watched her parents leave early in the morning, so excited to meet with the owner of the Theater Royale over the prospect of renting the venue for a concert of her father's music. By noon, Mrs. Lambert had rushed into the shop with the terrible news of the bridge collapse.

Olivia closed her eyes and drew a wavering breath. Her

mother. Gone. Her father, when they'd pulled him from the River Clyde, was barely alive. He'd suffered tremendous injuries, but by far the most grievous had been the blow to his head. For weeks, he'd hovered on the brink between life and death. A week after he opened his eyes, she'd realized the awful truth. He'd changed forever. His injury had rendered him childlike, forgetful in all concerns, with the exception of his music.

"Is that you, child?" Mrs. Lambert's deep voice called through the curtained doorway at the back of the shop.

Olivia straightened. "Yes, Mrs. Lambert. I will come straightway."

She glanced about. The small oil lamp on the edge of the back counter provided enough light to reveal the shop boy had, again, forgotten to sweep the floor. He'd also failed to straighten the sheaves of music on the shelves.

She scowled and tugged off her jacket. There would be little sleep for her this night. She pushed the curtain aside and hurried into the narrow hall, past the print room to the small parlor tucked at the very back of the shop.

The room was cozy. Her father's worktable took up the entire center of the room, its surface scattered with sheets of music, quills, and several inkpots. A large beeswax pillar candle burned bright in the very center of the room. Near the window, Mrs. Lambert sat in a blanket-covered, wing-backed chair.

At the back of the room, her father hunched over the piano keys, a wiry, spry man with spectacles balanced on the tip of his nose. His cap had fallen to the floor, and his injury lay bare for all to see. Even after all these years, the hair had not grown back over the scar.

Olivia scooped his cap from the floor. "Good evening, father." She dropped a kiss on the top of his head, then eased the knitted wool over his scars.

Her father glanced up with a smile. "Olivia, dear." His green eyes sparkled. "My, my, how you've grown, child."

The moments she shared with her father were so bittersweet. Since the accident, his greeting was always the same. Next, he'd ask about her mother.

"Now, where is your mother? 'Tis late." His brows knit in concern.

"She'll be along, Father." It wasn't really a lie. Within three minutes, he'd have forgotten what she said. She'd learned long ago to simply listen to the flow of his thoughts.

"What of Ralph? Do let him in, will you?"

Ralph, the terrier, had died the previous year. "I will, father," she promised. If she didn't distract him, he'd try to look for the dog himself. "You were playing a new tune when I came in. Play it again, will you?" She struck a few keys.

"I would be delighted, my dear." He laughed and ran his fingers over the keyboard, the music pulling him back into a safer world, a world of peace.

Olivia drew a breath.

"That'll be an extra tuppence, love. You were late."

Olivia glanced over at Mrs. Lambert, who sat darning a sock. She was a tall, middle-aged woman with gray-streaked hair pulled into such a severe bun that it made Olivia wince. Did the woman feel no pain? And while she browbeat her hair, so that not a single strand escaped its tight knot, she allowed the five straggly hairs sprouting from a large black mole on her chin to grow wither they willed.

"So, now I am owed two shillings proper." Mrs. Lambert gathered her darning and rose.

Olivia shook her head to clear her thoughts. "Right away, Mrs. Lambert."

"I had begun to fret, child." Mrs. Lambert clucked her reprimand.

"I am sorry, Mrs. Lambert. I didn't mean to inconvenience

you."

"Oh, it's no trouble, child." The woman's smile set the hairs on her mole jiggling. "Your father is a delight to listen to. He's talented, that man. Came up with a new song today. It's lovely, so very lovely."

Olivia smiled proudly. "I'll just hurry and fetch your coins, Mrs. Lambert." She picked up an unused candle from the top of the piano and lit the wick from the beeswax pillar.

"Will you need me in the morning?" Mrs. Lambert asked.

She nearly said no, then suddenly remembered Deborah's plea. "Yes, if you can. I do need to visit my cousin in the morning. I shan't be long."

"Then I will be here, straight after breakfast, love."

Olivia smiled. The woman might look like a gargoyle come to life, but Olivia had yet to meet a kinder soul.

The candle spat and guttered as Olivia hurried down the hall and into the print room. She lit the lamp, blew out the candle, and checked the shutters. Thankfully, they were closed and, although several slates were missing, the gaps were too small for a cat to slip through. Still, she glanced over the long, narrow counters and shelves lining the walls for Mr. Peppers, just in case. Either the cat wasn't there, or he'd disguised himself amidst the paper, type, and ink pots to watch her through evil eyes, waiting for her to leave before he wreaked havoc with the music.

A quick glance at the drying sheets of music revealed them to be arranged in slovenly rows and with several corners bent. She scowled. William took the lazy route with each task. Quickly, she straightened the pages, relieved to see crisp clean lines and staves with nary a cat pawprint in sight. She'd have William start on the bindings on the morrow—provided she didn't finish them before he arrived.

She squeezed past the large printing press in the center of the room and, with one last glance to assure she was alone, sank on her knees and reached for the loose floorboard. After several tugs, she dislodged it enough to reach into the hole and fish out the flat wooden box she'd wedged there.

Everything of importance in her life lay inside the box, from Louisa's contracts to her mother's locket, down to the very last coin she possessed—including the bent one. She opened the lid. Louisa's contracts lay folded on top. She winced, not wanting to think of Louisa anymore that night, and quickly set them aside. She picked up the small bag that contained her mother's locket and touched the green velvet to her lips. Even after almost four years, she had yet to look at the thing. The small money pouch lay at the bottom of the box. Each month, it felt lighter.

"No matter," she muttered. "Soon, you will be so plump, you will not fit." She snorted. If only that could be true.

Quickly, she untied the bag and shook a few shillings. The old, bent coin bounced off her fingers and onto the floor. She picked it up and dropped it into the bag. She'd vowed never to spend it until she had no choice, the last coin to stand between her and the streets.

Because Mrs. Lambert fretted over the authenticity of her coins, Olivia selected the two shiniest, then returned the box and its contents to its hiding place. After one last slam of her fist to assure the floorboard safely back in place, she stood.

A short time later, with Mrs. Lambert safely paid and sent home, and her father tucked into bed, she returned to the print room and began the tedious task of setting type.

It wasn't until the midnight hour chimed on the clock that she remembered the gray-eyed stranger in Lady Blair's garden. For a moment, she closed her eyes and relived his startling kiss in each glorious detail. Olivia grimaced, then she rolled her eyes.

The man was obviously a rake. The most handsome, charismatic men always were.

CHAPTER 3

Lord Nicholas Hunter Blair, 4th Baronet of Dunskey, watched Lord Chesterfield mop sweat from his brow. By George, the mam leaked like a sieve. He obviously had no business at the gaming table, not when he clearly fretted over the sum he'd just lost and that which he stood only seconds away from losing, as well.

A soft pair of hands slid over Nicholas's shoulders and a sultry voice whispered in his ear, "Are you coming up to bed soon?"

It was Demelza. If truth be told, he wasn't in the mood for her attentions, even though he'd already paid for her particular skills a week in advance. He glanced around the bordello's card room, strangely restless. Something had roiled inside him the entire day, a something he had yet to identify. Something that informed him that he didn't want to be here.

He cocked a brow at his winning hand of cards. Whatever disturbed him hadn't affected his game—but then, nothing usually did. Lady Luck had taken a fancy to him, one that had lasted nearly a decade. She'd tucked him safely in her bosom and handed him wins, worth twice over his inheritance. Easily.

He certainly didn't need to torture a man over a paltry two hundred pounds.

As fresh beads of sweat sprouted along Lord Chesterfield's hairline, Nicholas cleared his throat and dropped his cards on the table.

"What say we end the game here, eh?" he drawled with a lazy yawn. "Let's call it done. I am in the mood for...other things."

Lord Chesterfield's eyes widened and his face split with relief.

"Upstairs, my lord?" Demelza thrust her breasts forward.

Nicholas lifted himself to his feet and eyed the mass of blonde curls so artfully arranged over an exquisite, creamy expanse of skin. Her dress hung only an inch or two from falling off her curvaceous form entirely, but inexplicably, his body only offered a tepid, half-hearted response before abandoning the effort altogether.

How odd. Had he tired of Demelza so soon? Or was it—

Red. He chuckled, and knew what ailed him.

A particularly eye-catching shade of red hair, one he'd seen just that afternoon, in his mother's garden. It was the lass who had surprised him with a kiss that played on his mind. Was she an opera singer, as well? The thought intrigued him. Opera singers made worthy mistresses. By far, his most unforgettable lover had been Florinda Marie de Bussonne, the Lark of Paris. There were times, still, that he was half-tempted to cross the channel and return to her bed.

"My lord?" Demelza leaned forward and offered him a fine view of her breasts, the silk gown so low as to half reveal her nipples.

Truthfully, he'd enjoyed the snug, tantalizing fit of the garden redhead's lacy, light muslin far more. Though far less revealing than Demelza's gown, the play of the lass's cloth had teased his senses, drawing him into the world of fantasy—a world that sent a spike of arousal straight through him.

A dark blue ribbon had spanned the redhead's bodice, running a satin circle just under her ample breasts. Just what would she look like, wearing that ribbon…and nothing else?

"My lord?"

He expelled a breath and, now more than ready, followed Demelza up the stairs.

Once in the room, he sprawled back on the bed, closed his eyes and envisioned quite another lass who unbuttoned his trousers, another pair of lips on his hardening flesh. Teasing. Nipping. Sucking.

Then, the heat of Demelza's mouth consumed him, and he thought no more.

CHAPTER 4

THE LARGE BAY WINDOW WITH ITS FINE VIEW OF A TIDY ROSE garden dominated the Duke of Lennox's parlor. Olivia scarcely noticed the tasteful green velvet settee and matching chairs, the pictures suspended on brass chains, and the grandfather clock in the corner.

As she stepped into the room, a sound to her left made her turn. Deborah sat curled up in a window seat. She wore a lavender gown edged with an ivory-colored Brussels bobbin lace and held a book. She was surrounded by so many brightly colored pillows that Olivia couldn't help but think she looked like a nervous hen, sitting on a nest. The comparison only deepened when Deborah dropped her book with a strangled squawk and then jumped to her feet, sending the cushions flying in all directions. A gold-fringed bolster rolled to stop at Olivia's feet.

"You came," Deborah gasped.

"Of course." Olivia smiled.

Deborah lunged and threw her arms around Olivia's waist, buried her brown ringlets against Olivia's shoulder and began to sob.

"What is it?" Olivia asked, alarmed. "What happened?"

"Whatever shall I do?" Deborah wailed.

As she sobbed, Olivia patted her shoulder, and eventually managed to guide her back to the window seat.

"Dry your tears and tell me." Olivia gave her cousin's hands a comforting squeeze. "Whatever upsets you, I am sure we can solve it together."

Deborah's elfin face contorted. "I do not think so," she gulped.

"Come, now. How bad can it be?"

"Oh, Olivia, whatever shall I do? Heaven help me, tongues will wag, soon, about the thickness of my waist."

Olivia sat down by her side and gave her knee a comforting pat. "Please, Deborah, tell me what it is so I may help you."

Deborah passed her hands over her face, then turned her head away. After several long moments, she whispered, "You are so strong, Olivia. You aren't afraid of anyone, are you?"

That wasn't true, but now was hardly the time to disagree. "Afraid? Are you afraid of someone?"

Deborah closed her eyes and blurted, "I am with child." The words were scarcely out of her mouth before her lashes flew open and she clamped a hand over her mouth, as if surprised at her own confession.

Olivia simply stared as the word slowly registered. Her mouth gaped. "A chi—"

"Hush." Deborah flinched and then quickly placed a finger over Olivia's lips. "Do not say it. Not a word."

Olivia's brows rose, her eyes drawn like a magnet to her cousin's slender waistline before she forced her gaze back to her face. "Are you certain?"

As a fresh onslaught of tears cascaded down Deborah's cheeks, Olivia could only assume the reaction meant 'yes.'

"What of the father?" Olivia asked. "Surely, he asked you to wed him?" Obviously, he hadn't. Otherwise, Deborah would be discussing her wedding plans, instead.

Deborah averted her gaze. "Nae," she replied, her voice managing to quaver three octaves within the single syllable alone.

A red-hot wave of anger rolled over Olivia. "The *cad*. Tell me, who is this man?"

"I can't." Debora's shoulders sagged.

"I insist."

Deborah whirled to face her. "Why? Why must you know?"

"Why? *Why?* I will demand he do the honorable thing," Olivia retorted. "He must wed you. At *once*."

Deborah sniffed, clearly locked in her misery.

Olivia forced a calming breath and slowly reigned in her temper. "You asked me to come here, didn't you? Let me help you. Please, Deborah."

Deborah hesitated, then squeezed her fingers.

"Tell me who he is," Olivia urged.

Still, at least a minute passed before Deborah finally whispered with a rush, "Nicholas."

"Nicholas?" Olivia repeated with an encouraging smile. "Nicholas who?"

Deborah squirmed and replied even softer this time, "Lord Nicholas Blair."

"Ah, Lady Blair's son?" Olivia nodded thoughtfully.

From what she'd heard of the man, the behavior certainly matched. He was a rake to the bone, but he was no match for her. After dealing with bankers for nearly four years, taking a rake to task would be nothing.

Olivia stood, strode to the writing desk, and picked up a sheet of paper.

"Whatever are you doing?" Deborah asked from the window seat.

"I shall inform Lord Blair to act with honor." She reached

for the quill. "I will impress upon him that a man takes responsibility—"

"No, no, not *that*," Deborah gasped. She flew across the room and snatched the quill from Olivia's grasp. "Let's not tell anyone. *I beg you.*"

Olivia blinked, surprised, and again, her eyes fell to Deborah's waist. "This is not a matter that can wait, I would think. The man should be held *responsible*. Surely, your grandfather—"

"Save me," Deborah wailed as she wilted to the floor. "He will disown me, Olivia. I am...*ruined*."

"Not if Nicholas lives up to his responsibility," Olivia reminded doggedly.

Deborah covered her face with her hands as the tears flowed.

A sudden knock on the door startled them both.

Deborah jumped to her feet and choked, "Enter."

The maid entered. If she noticed Deborah's tear reddened face, she gave no indication of it. "His Grace requests your presence in his study, Miss Mackenzie."

Olivia raised her brows. Whatever did the man want? An apology for her behavior at the garden party? If so, he'd be sorely disappointed.

"Very well."

Deborah reached for her hand, her eyes pleading for her silence.

"Do not fret." Olivia gave her fingers a hearty squeeze. "We shall think of something."

She followed the maid down the red Turkish-carpeted stairs to a large wood-paneled door.

"Enter," a deep voice boomed in response to the maid's sharp rap.

The maid opened the door and stood aside. Olivia entered. The comforting scent of leather stood at direct odds with the menacing figure of her grandfather seated behind a massive mahogany desk. One look at his thick brows drawn into a disapproving line and Olivia revolted again at the thought of curtseying. She couldn't even bring her lips to utter the courtesy of 'my lord,' much less, 'your grace.' Nae, not even a 'sir.' She was not a performing animal to dance to his tune.

After all, what could he do? Disown her? Suppressing a snort, she looked him straight in the eye. The duke's eyes narrowed perceptibly, taking in her simple gown and work-roughened, ink-smudged hands. She arched a brow. She had nothing to hide nor was she ashamed.

"Sit." He nodded his chin at the leather chair before his desk.

She took the seat and waited. A gleam entered his eye, but since she didn't know the man, she had no idea what that gleam might mean.

"Lady Blair has informed me of this concert nonsense," he said.

Ah, he was angry.

"*An Enchanted Summer Evening* is hardly nonsense," she disagreed with a shrug.

"A proper lady does *not* sponsor questionable events." The craggy lines of his face deepened into a frown. "Nor does a lady keep close company with *opera singers*," he spat the words in distaste.

After that glimpse into Louisa's drawing room, Olivia could well see his point, but at the moment, she'd rather die than agree. "Then, it is fortunate I am not a proper lady," she said with a toss of her head.

"You are my granddaughter," he grated.

"Am I?" She didn't attempt to hold back the snort this time. "How strange. We only just met. Is there proof?"

"You have an insolent mouth on you," he snapped.

"Because I dare speak the truth?" she challenged with a frosty smile. "Frankly, you have no power over me."

"Is that so?"

"Yes."

They locked gazes.

Finally, he sat back in his chair and dropped a hand on each leather-studded arm with a distinct slap. "Give up this foolish venture, and I will bestow upon you a suitable dowry."

So, he thought to buy her. "You fear for your reputation that much, then?"

"Do not let your pride stand in the way of a good match, girl."

Girl. To him, she was just a 'girl,' but someone who could harm his reputation, damage his ego with gossip. What a fool. She held the power in their relationship—not him. She stood. "I do not need your help."

The duke stared at her, astonished. "You would refuse a dowry? The chance to find a decent husband?"

A husband would make her dealings with the bank easier—if she were to find one malleable enough, one who would aid her dreams and not destroy them. She'd thought Timothy to be such a one, but apparently, he'd lacked a spine, altogether. Now, she knew in her heart, she'd be better off dealing with the bank alone. She didn't need to complicate her life with a husband.

"Aye," she said with a small laugh at her newfound understanding. "I will do much better on my own."

The duke's nostrils flared. "You are as headstrong and hot-tempered as your mother."

Olivia raised her chin. "Why, thank you. That's the first compliment you have bestowed upon me."

He rose, tall and stern. He placed his palms flat on the desk and leaned forward, looking very much like a bird of prey. "Do not be a fool," he hissed. "Your mother lost everything because of pride. Did she not tell you of the Blue Slipper?"

The sapphire encrusted symbol of inheritance, her mother's

by birth. With the Blue Slipper in her mother's hands, she would have been named the Duchess of Lennox.

With a proud toss of her head, Olivia hissed in return, "My mother had no need for such empty, useless trinkets."

"You would call the Duchy of Lennox a trinket?" His lip curled in disdain.

"Absolutely. What is all the wealth in the world without love?" Olivia's lip curled to match. Leaning over the desk herself, she thrust her ink-stained hand beneath his nose. "I do not need your help. Look at my fingers. They are *my* prize. I know well how to take care of myself."

He stared at her, his face an unreadable mask. No doubt, fury beyond measure boiled in him. She shrugged. She didn't care. He and his titles meant nothing to her.

"I bid you good day." She left him, huffing and puffing, and sailed out the door.

No wonder Deborah was distraught.

Their grandfather was an obstinate, judgmental prig.

THE DAY WAS A WARM AND PLEASANT ONE. NOT A CLOUD MARRED the sky as Olivia crossed the road and took the tree-lined paths of Glasgow Green. Lost in thought, she scarcely heard the birds chirping from the treetops as she walked alongside the River Clyde.

Deborah *must* have heard of Lord Blair's reputation. Why hadn't she exercised caution in his company? Surely, the man could not be *that* intriguing—not with a reputation of that caliber to precede him.

Truly, she knew only one way to help her cousin.

She would take up the matter directly with Lord Nicholas Blair herself.

CHAPTER 5

Nicholas balanced his chair on its two back legs in the dimly lit card room. He scarcely noticed the cards in his hand. He had women on his mind. Two, to be exact—opposites in the extreme.

Foremost was the chit, Olivia. Deborah's cousin. The harridan who had authored the letter that had dragged him from his friend's house party in Culzean Castle, and back down to Glasgow. What had she called him? Ah, yes, a spineless coward and a scoundrel absconding responsibility for the pursuit of pleasure, a man thinking more with his base parts than with his brain.

He winced. The words hit closer to home than he cared to admit—especially since he couldn't stop thinking of the redhead he'd kissed in his mother's garden. Since he'd left Wedderburn Manor, he'd wanted no one else. Now *there* was a tempting vixen, a bonny, unforgettable lass, one entirely different from Deborah's shrew of a cousin.

"Abandon?" Lord Fredrick's voice boomed through his thoughts. "Play?"

Nicholas glanced up.

Lord Fredrick sat across the table puffing his cheroot in long, vigorous pulls. The thin wisps of smoke spiraled over his head in mesmerizing circles, calling Nicholas back to his thoughts like a siren. By George, he'd never touched Deborah in his life. He hadn't even seen the lass in two years—maybe longer. Even then, she'd never caught his eye. He didn't care for the timid types. He liked his women capricious, strong-willed, surprising. Nae, Deborah was too timorous to dream up this mad scheme. This was clearly the work of her cousin—no doubt, she wanted to extort him.

"Which is it, lad? Abandon or play?" Lord Fredrick's voice held a hint of dry amusement.

Nicholas flipped his cards with his thumb, slammed his chair down, then dropped his hand on the table with a grunt. A chuckle circled the table.

"You've lost again, Blair."

"You're off your game. Oh, that I have lived to see the day."

Nicholas exhaled through his nose. Devil take it, had he really lost again? That made every game of Three-Card Loo that night. He stood and cocked a brow at the mahogany paneling closing around him. He felt trapped. Surprisingly, not by the chit who had authored the scathing letter, but by the sheer monotony of the endless parties, the card games, and even the vapid women with whom he kept company.

A bagpipe blared an Irish reel on the other side of the tavern's backroom door. A wave of laughter followed, along with the thump of dancing feet. Simple pleasures. A song. A dance. A woman, hearth, and home. Children.

Damnation. What was he thinking? For the first time, he noticed the men around the table, watching him in overt amusement.

"You have a woman on your mind now, haven't you?" Lord Fredrick chuckled and took another puff on his cheroot.

Nicholas shrugged. "Good evening, gentlemen."

A footman handed him his hat and coat at the door. Then, he left the card room, pushed through the throng of dancers and out into the crisp, night air.

"A ride, my lord?" a man called from a parked coach. "Two shillings to Parsonage Square."

Nicholas shook his head and turned down the darkened street. He was a block away from his residence of choice whenever he stayed in Glasgow: Madame Prescott's House of Pleasure. Almost two weeks had come and gone since he'd last enjoyed Demelza's company.

The maid saw him coming and opened the door.

"You have returned, my lord." Demelza flew to him from the stairs.

She ran her hands over his shoulders, just as he liked, yet strangely, even more than the last time, he felt no response. Perhaps he was just tired.

"A game of cards?" she asked. "Wine? Whisky?"

Nicholas yawned. "Bed."

Her trademark sultry smile played over her lips.

He followed her up the stairs, dimly aware of her sashaying hips preceding him. She teased him, of course, but he had other concerns. He planned to visit Olivia first thing in the morning. After all, he could scarcely show up at the duke's residence to inquire about the matter of Deborah's pregnancy. Real or not, it wouldn't matter. The duke, her grandfather, would behead him first and ask questions later.

Afterwards, he'd pay a visit to his mother. Doubtless, she'd know the identity of the mysterious beauty he'd kissed in the garden. The corner of his lip lifted in a smile as he felt himself harden. The thought of her, even nearly two weeks later, sent a shiver of arousal through him. Clearly, he was smitten. They reached the room.

"My lord," Demelza turned and reached for his trousers.

He inhaled and yawned, then brushed her probing hands

away with an irritated sweep of his hand, stalked to the bed and fell across the counterpane, face down.

"My lord?" Demelza queried.

The mattress dipped as she joined him. She pulled at his shoulders until he rolled onto his back. She'd let her gown fall to her waist, but the sight of her naked breasts did little to excite him. Her lips puckered in a pout, as she ran her hands over his chest.

"What's this?" She withdrew Olivia's letter from his inner waistcoat pocket.

He grunted. "A lie."

"A lie?" She arched a finely plucked brow.

Unbidden, she opened the parchment and read aloud.

HONORABLE SIR,

IT IS MY DUTY TO INFORM YOU OF A MATTER YOU MUST *immediately set to rights. My cousin, Deborah Hay, has informed me of a delicate matter that you must address with the utmost urgency, and in order to assure there are no misunderstandings, I must come, at once and with unnatural candor, to the point.*

Deborah is expecting your child. You must discharge your duty and...

"ARGH," NICHOLAS GROWLED, AND SWATTED THE LETTER FROM her hand.

"Is it true?" Demelza ran her fingers over his body.

"Nae," he grunted. "Not a word of it."

"Oh?" Demelza tilted her head to the side. "You have been so distracted of late. Quite unlike yourself."

So, she'd noticed. He shrugged and yawned again. "I am tired."

"Men do not come here to sleep, my lord." She slid her fingers into his trousers.

He lay still, again experiencing a decided lack of interest to the painted woman's attempts to arouse him. Clearly, his body had decided to mutiny at the prospect of Demelza's charms for even a night. He'd obviously outgrown his fascination with her.

In the morning, he'd have to find a hotel. Perhaps, they would finished building that new one by the river...his horse would appreciate the stables there, far more than the brothel's cramped accommodations. No doubt, they would employ better stable hands, as well. He'd ridden his finest red roan from Culzean Castle. Such a horse needed daily exercise, a proper stretching of the legs.

Dimly, he noted that Demelza had increased her vigor, trying her best to spark his interest. He yawned, yet again. He could always return to the King's Arms, a quaint establishment that housed the Hunter's Club, his favorite card room in Glasgow—not that he'd been particularly interested in cards, of late, either.

He winced at Demelza's ministrations. By George, she would bloody soon rub him raw if he didn't put them both out their misery. Closing his eyes, he summoned again the image of the mysterious, auburn-haired lass. His cock lifted at once.

Demelza moaned in relief. Caught in his fantasy, he thrust his cock gently between her lips until he'd hardened enough. Without bothering to undress further, he took her quickly, his mind still on quite another shapely form. To his surprise, he spilled his seed in less than a dozen strokes. As usual, Demelza faked her pleasure, one perfectly timed to coincide with his. Only gold or silver baubles or a five-pound note could elicit a true response.

He rose. She slithered over the counterpane and grasped his

manhood, then sucked the tip as he withdrew a fifty-pound note from his inner waistcoat pocket. A gleam of true pleasure lit her eyes as he pulled himself free.

"My lord." She grabbed the note as if he might change his mind.

He tucked his manhood away and buttoned his trousers. Then, he picked up the letter from the floor.

"You are not staying?" Demelza asked.

"Nae." He strode to the door.

"You're not coming back." It was a statement, not a question.

He dropped his hand on the knob.

"I will miss you, my lord."

She wouldn't miss *him*. She'd miss his money. He didn't mind, of course. It was their agreed upon arrangement and she'd relieved him well enough, for a time. Now, he wanted something much more. He wanted the hunt, the challenge of coaxing a lass into his bed—a lass who might stay there for a lifetime…and not just any lass. He knew the one he wanted.

First, he needed to set Deborah's scheming cousin to rights.

CHAPTER 6

Louisa sang like an angel, but Olivia couldn't enjoy a single note. Her thoughts whirled in endless circles as she sat in the very last row of the Theater Royale's mezzanine. The print shop roof had sprung another leak during the night. That made four now. She grimaced. She'd have to climb up and mend the roof tiles herself. She couldn't afford a roofer.

On the stage, Louisa belted her aria. The stage lights caught on the glass beads sewn onto her dress, making her glisten like a star. Olivia glanced around at the enraptured audience and permitted herself a small smile. They were so entranced, they would insist on at least two encores—both of which Olivia had contracted Louisa to sing, *The Soldier's Adieu* and *Fly Swiftly, Ye Moments*. The songs were new, popular, and as yet, she was the only music publishing house to carry them. They would sell well.

Finally, Louisa shrilled the last note and the large, red velvet curtain dropped, signaling the start of intermission.

Olivia rose from her seat and descended the marble stairs leading into the opera house lobby. Halfway down, she paused with her hand on the brass railing and surveyed the small groups of elegantly clad women and men as they chatted under the pendant chandelier. So many potential customers. With a bright smile, she joined them and wound her way through the crowd.

She'd just dropped what must have been her fiftieth hint that Mackenzie Publishing House kept a wide variety of sheet music for the musically inclined when she heard her name.

"Olivia! Olivia, child."

Olivia turned to see Lady Blair standing under a large, gilt framed mirror and waving her fan. Dressed in a dark burgundy satin gown with a matching turban and a strand of pearls clasped about her neck, she exuded an unmatchable air of grace and elegance.

Olivia smiled and hurried to her side, but she'd only closed the distance halfway when she suddenly remembered her letter. Heavens, what if her rake of a son had told her what she'd written? She tripped as a thread of alarm snaked through her.

"Olivia? What is it, child?" A flare of concern crossed Lady Blair's face. "You look as if you've seen a ghost."

Olivia bobbed a quick curtsey. "Forgive me, my lady. I was simply lost in thought." She searched Lady Blair's face for any sign of displeasure, but to her great relief, found none.

"Lost in thought, child? I must admit, you do seem rather distracted." Lady Blair's eyes took on a sly, hopeful expression. "May I inquire the nature?"

Olivia suppressed a snort. She recognized that look. As ever, Lady Blair sought to play the role of the matchmaker. "I fear I will only disappoint you in that regard," she replied.

Few men desired a wife who understood a printing press better than how to dance a quadrille.

"Do come visit Wedderburn, will you, child?" Lady Blair gave her arm a warm squeeze. "My son will be here tomorrow. I would so dearly love the two of you to meet."

Olivia shifted uneasily. Tomorrow? Hopefully, his return signaled his plan to make things right with Deborah. Lord above, she could only pray he'd keep her part in the matter to himself.

"That would be lovely, my lady." She forced a smile. "If you will excuse me, I must be going. Duty calls."

Lady Blair smiled in approval. "You do your father credit, child. I wish you the best of luck. Please, when you return home, give him my greetings."

This time, the smile curving Olivia's lips was genuine as she ducked away.

The bell chimed shortly after, signaling the end of intermission and Olivia returned to her seat. Again, Louisa delivered a flawless performance, and again, Olivia paid little heed. Time flew, and before she thought possible, Louisa lay dying on the stage, warbling her last solo as the women in the audience sniffed emotionally behind their fans.

Finally, the last note died away, and the audience rose to applaud, Olivia among them. Again and again, they called Louisa back on stage until at last, she smoothed her skirts for the encore. The piano began to play, but by the third note, Olivia's heart began to pound. Louisa was singing the wrong song. Why?

As the strains of Moore's *When Love Is Kind* filled the opera house, Olivia began to panic. She didn't have Moore's score, nor any sheet music of the song. Only James Rotherham's publishing house still carried the song. She clenched her fingers into fists. When her customers arrived in the morning to discover she hadn't a single sheet printed, they would think her a liar. Her reputation would be ruined.

As Louisa began the second verse, Olivia leapt from her seat, dashed down the stairs, and headed down the hallway to the back of the opera house. Nausea roiled her stomach. She couldn't afford another financial blunder, not with the final concert payment due—as well as the payments for the ink and printing press repairs. The pending loss of sales would be a devastating blow to her already fragile position.

She bit her lip and charged around the corner. To her surprise, a burly, red-faced man with a crooked nose lounged against the door leading to the back of the stage.

"If you will excuse me?" Olivia huffed.

He crossed his arms and peered down at her with a grin. "You must be Miss Olivia?"

Olivia raised a haughty brow. "Have we met?"

He eyed her boldly, then dropped his head close to hers. "We could have, if you like." The faint stench of rotten fish rolled over her face.

Olivia stepped back. "Move out of my way," she ordered with a stern glare. She'd met plenty of his kind. All bark and no bite.

She took another step toward the door, fully expecting him to stand aside. To her shock, he grabbed her arm instead.

"Mistress Hamilton doesn't wish to see you, lass—but I can't say the same."

"Unhand me. At once." She tried to wrench free of his hold.

"Let the lass go," a man's cool voice ordered sharply from behind.

The burly man released Olivia like a hot potato. Olivia exhaled and stepped back as Lord Randall stepped into view, looking neat and suave in a black coat with an intricately tied white cravat, a fine pair of dark gray breeches and the curl of his silver-handled walking stick hooked lazily over his muscular arm.

"Good evening, Miss Mackenzie." He reached for her hand and lifted her fingers gently to his lips, his silver cufflinks glittering in the hallway's dim lamplight. "I trust you are well?"

She wouldn't be if Louisa barged through the door and saw Lord Randall paying attention to her once again.

She snatched back her hand. "I am fine, thank you."

He smiled. "Perhaps, may I be of service?"

Olivia hesitated, torn between leaving and speaking with Louisa. There still might be one more encore, a chance to correct the error. "I must speak with Louisa, my lord. I shan't keep her long."

Lord Randall frowned. "You seem to suffer a misunderstanding, Miss Mackenzie. Miss Hamilton's time is no concern of mine." He paused, then added with a rueful smile, "I fear I was rather drunk when we last met at her evening party. My behavior was not the best. Please, accept my apologies."

Miss Hamilton's time is no concern of mine? Somehow, Olivia didn't think Louisa would agree, not when she'd gushed over the man for weeks.

"Am I forgiven?" Lord Randall pressed.

Why did the glint in his eye remind her of a hawk? And why did she feel like the prey? "Of course, my lord. Think no more of the matter."

Judging by the rounds of applause from the hall, it was already too late. Damnation. She had to find some way to soothe Louisa's ruffled feathers before she ended up in the poorhouse. The woman had broken her contract and sung the wrong encore songs out of spite. It was a blow, assuredly. She had to make sure the matter ended there. She didn't dare even *think* of what might happen should Louisa refuse to participate in *An Enchanted Evening*, as well.

"I will have my carriage brought around to the back," Lord Randall's voice interrupted her thoughts.

And have Louisa see her in his carriage? Olivia snorted. "Good evening, my lord," she said firmly. "If you will excuse me, I must be going."

She didn't wait for his reply. He called her name, but the sound only lent an extra urgency to her step as she bolted out the back door and out into the pleasant spring evening.

She didn't live far away, just across Glasgow Green. The voices of the opera house patrons mingled with the clip clop of hooves, filling the night air, as Olivia crossed the street and took the river path leading into the park.

She hurried under the bright moon, the light more than enough to guide her way. Her thoughts spun in worried circles, but gradually, the soothing murmur of the River Clyde calmed her mind, and by the time she emerged from under the trees, she had the beginnings of a plan.

First thing in the morning, she would visit James Rotherham and Lewis Prescott, music publishers, both. They had, on occasion, assisted her father in the past, and even though she suspected Prescott of secretly wishing failure upon her ventures, she had no choice but to ask if she could borrow the score of Moore's *When Love Is Kind*. How could they refuse if she shared the profits? If William rushed to set the type, she *might* be able to print enough to satisfy her most loyal customers before they arrived.

Of course, she still had other monies due, but she would solved those before by paying higher fees. The only true issue that remained would be paying Mr. Pitt of the Theatre Royale. Olivia winced. She'd never sell herself to the man. *Never*.

The shop bell jingled as she slipped through the door and, as ever, she paused to let the sounds of her father's piano soothe her troubled mind.

"How were the sales?" Mrs. Lambert asked as Olivia stepped into the parlor.

Olivia faked a bright smile. "Promising," she replied. It was true. The sales were promising—providing she could print the goods.

She crossed to where her father hunched over the piano, his fingers flying over the keys.

"Olivia," he greeted warmly. "My, child, how you've grown."

"Yes, Papa," she murmured.

"And your mother?" he asked, lifting his fingers from the keys.

Gently, Olivia placed his hands back on the piano. "That's a lovely tune, Father. Is it new?"

He smiled absently. "Why, yes. It reminds me of your mother on a spring day."

Then, just like that, the music swept him away, once again. It was easy—too easy. Olivia suppressed a sigh.

"Will you need me in the morning, child?" Mrs. Lambert asked as Olivia dropped the shillings onto her outstretched palm.

With so much work to be done, she would need her help the entire day. "Please, Mrs. Lambert. I would be grateful."

The woman and her mole hairs nodded. She tucked the coins into her pocket, then paused. "You're a good lass, Olivia. Someday, your luck will change. My bones tell me this is so."

Olivia could only hope. "Thank you, Mrs. Lambert."

She watched her vanish into the night, then closed and locked the door.

For a moment, she leaned her forehead against the wood and closed her eyes. If only she could turn back time and become a child once again, a child with both a mother *and* a father. Of course, it was impossible. Perhaps, she could find a husband to love, instead. A man who would accept her father and support her dream of publishing his music to the world. The thought pulled a bitter laugh from her lips. The first dream was more likely than the second. With a snort, she headed to the print room to ready the press.

Tomorrow would be a busy day. She had publishers to visit and hopefully music to print. As for Louisa, she'd have to pay her a visit—a long overdue one.

THE NEXT MORNING, OLIVIA SAILED INTO THE PRINT SHOP, irritated. Lewis Prescott had lent her the score. He'd even sold her a packet of paper—but at a steep price *and* he'd demanded half the profits. She stripped off her gloves and glanced around the shop. Empty. Not a customer in sight. Even worse, she saw neither hide nor hair of the shop boy.

She slammed the basket of paper on the counter. "William? William?" She paused and raised her voice, "William?"

On the third call, William stumbled through the curtains at the back of the shop, rubbing sleep from his eyes with ink-stained hands. He was a lanky lad with a shock of brown hair and a large gap between his two front teeth that lent a whistle to his speech.

"Where have you been?" Olivia seethed. "If I had been a thief, I could have walked off with everything here whilst you slept."

William winced. "I didn't hear the bell, Miss," he swore, the word 'miss' sounding more like 'mithhhst.' "Not once, all morning long."

Olivia bristled. If true, it was the worst of news. "It is more likely you slept through the customers that came calling." She could only hope—and hope they would return.

He had the grace to look guilty.

She drummed her fingers on the packet of paper resting on the counter. In her father's time, the papermakers had delivered endless boxes of the smooth, creamy sheets, collecting their fees once, at the end of the month. Now, she had to pay twice the price and first, before she even made a single print.

"Have you made the ink?"

The lad scratched his nose.

Olivia gritted her teeth. "Go. Now. We have work to do."

He dove behind the curtains before she could twist his ear.

Olivia growled under her breath. The sound of her father's piano filtered in from the back of the shop. At least he was happy. She heaved a sigh and divesting herself of her hat and pelisse, grabbed an apron and headed for the print room.

By the end of the hour, she stood over the frames with a sense of satisfaction, inspecting each bar line, musical symbol, and stave thrice over.

"They're ready." She dusted her hands and turned to where she'd expected William to be.

Again, there was no sign of him. She scowled. She couldn't afford to pay him anymore, not when he offered her not a smidgeon of work in return.

The bell on the shop door jingled. Perhaps, the customers had come, at last? Eagerly, she hurried to the front. Pushing the curtain aside, she peered into the shop.

A man, his broad shoulders covered by a finely tailored navy coat with silver shanked buttons. She grinned. A customer—and a rich one, at that.

Dusting her skirts, she stepped into the room. "Good afternoon, my lord."

Her heart stilled. She'd quite forgotten him, but now that he stood before her again, every delicious detail of their kiss flooded her mind.

It was the blond-haired stranger from Lady Blair's garden party.

CHAPTER 7

Nicholas stepped down from his carriage and eyed the narrow townhouse with a censorious eye. Clearly, the place had seen better days. Rust pitted its black iron fencing and he could barely make out the writing on the weathered sign above the door: Mackenzie and Sons, Purveyors of Fine Music.

Removing his hat, he stepped inside. He heard the notes of a piano first, drifting through the curtains at the back of the shop. The pleasant scent of cedar assaulted his nostrils next. He glanced around. The simple shop held little more than boxes of sheet music, as expected, but nearly half stood empty. Still, despite its rundown condition, the place held a kind of charm. Oddly. And despite the harsh, venomous soul living there.

The curtains rustled at the back. He turned as a lass emerged. He recognized her, at once. The auburn-haired lass he'd kissed in his mother's garden. She froze, her eyes wide with surprise, and his lips curved with astonished delight.

She was even more fetching than he recalled, dressed in a high-waisted day dress made of a violet-sprigged muslin and a satin ribbon tied snug beneath her breasts. She'd swept her hair back in a loose bun, but a strand had escaped to curl at the nape of her neck—a neck he'd soon be nibbling if everything went as planned. Was that a smudge of ink on her chin? Her skin was white, without a freckle in sight—such an unusual combination with the redness of her hair.

"How *ever* did you find me?" A faint flush stained her cheekbones.

He stood, grinning like a fool for Lord knew how long, then the purpose of his visit paraded across his mind.

"I have a wee matter of business to settle, lass, and then I am at your disposal." Indeed, there was no rush to visit his mother any longer when the object of his desire stood before him. "I am looking for Olivia Mackenzie."

He glanced around, half expecting to see the old biddy charge through the curtains at the mere mention of her name.

The charming lass frowned. "What matter of business have you to settle with me?" she asked, her tone curious.

The words took much longer to register than they should have. When they did, they felt like a slap in the face.

The *redhead* had penned the letter?

Nicholas's playful mood vanished. Slowly, he retrieved the letter from his waistcoat pocket and dropped it on the counter.

"I am Nicholas. Nicholas Hunter Blair." He enunciated each syllable in chillier and chillier tones.

He watched the progression of emotions cross her face. Confusion, recognition, and then anger. Anger? The *chit*.

"You?" She swallowed hard.

With a derisive curl of his lip, he raised a brow, waved a hand at his surroundings. and with more acid than was his wont, stated, "At least, the motive is clear now."

Olivia's fine nostrils flared. "Pardon?"

"Shall I spell it out?" he asked.

"Please do," she hissed.

He slammed his palms flat on the counter. "You are blackmailing me to save your business, are you not? Have music sales soured of late?"

The shock and anger that flooded her face summoned such a sense of guilt that he almost apologized right then and there —despite the fact *he* was the innocent one.

"So, holding a man accountable to his responsibilities is deemed blackmail in your eyes?" she snapped with a fierce toss of her head.

By God, she was beautiful when she was angry. Those lips could tempt a man into ignoring his better judgment. He unwittingly leaned closer, but as he did so, the curtains behind the counter parted.

A wiry, gray-haired man entered the shop, his brows drawn into a faint line of confusion. "Good day, my lord," he addressed Nicholas with a bow. "How may I be of service? What music might you be looking for today?"

Before Nicholas could respond, Olivia shushed him with a warning scowl, then took the man by the arm.

"I am helping him, father," she said in a soft voice. "There is no cause for concern. Let's go back now, shall we?" Gently, she pulled him back toward the curtain.

The man peered down at her and his green eyes lit with amusement. "I swear, lass, have you grown since this morning?"

"I do believe I have, Father. Now, why don't you work on your music? I can take care of the customers."

The sadness that tinged her smile unexpectedly tugged Nicholas's heart.

"Customers?" The man's face lit, and he turned back to Nicholas. He bowed. "Goody day, my lord. How may I be of service? What music might you be looking for today?"

Nicholas narrowed his eyes as Olivia commandeered her father's arm and, this time, succeeded in pulling him through the curtain.

Odd. The man clearly suffered a malady of the memory. He wondered as to the cause as he glanced around the shop again, this time viewing the worn state of the place through a different pair of eyes. The lass was obviously struggling to make ends meet.

Shame flooded through him. He'd behaved as the worse kind of cad. He wasn't one to chide the helpless—despite her chosen method of digging herself out of her situation.

The soft tinkling of the piano resumed and a moment later, the curtains parted and Olivia returned. By God, there was something about the way she moved. He couldn't stop his eyes from dipping over the soft swell of her breasts and the curves of her hips as she marched to the counter.

"Where were we, my lord? I do believe you were accusing me of blackmail?" she snapped.

Had he thought her helpless? His lip twitched. She was as helpless as a viper. Why did that make his blood boil even more?

"I have been hasty in my judgment." He summoned his most charming smile. "I do apologize. I have no excuse."

Olivia lifted a suspicious brow.

"Surely, you can understand. What man enjoys a false accusation—" he began.

"False?" she interrupted with a snort.

She was a feisty one. A strange combination of irritation, admiration and lust flooded him. "I never laid a finger on your cousin Debora," he clipped, the irritation winning.

"You lie, then, sir. She bears your child."

"Deborah may very well be with child—but certainly not mine."

Olivia's green eyes widened. "Impossible."

"How so?" Nicholas challenged.

She scowled. "My cousin wouldn't lie over such a matter."

"She wouldn't be the first woman who did under such

circumstances," he observed in a dry tone. "As much as you may not wish to hear this, my dear, even I cannot father a child with a woman I haven't seen in nearly two years."

The long line of her lashes fluttered in surprise and, for several heartbeats, only the strains of the piano from the back room could be heard.

Then, clearly unwilling to abandon a fight, Olivia stubbornly raised her chin as if that settled the matter and said firmly, "Nae. Deborah wouldn't lie to me. We're... family."

Her words pulled a mocking laugh from his lips. "Then all the more reason to do so," he murmured dryly.

The lass thinned her lips in displeasure, and suddenly, he found himself drowning in the depths of her stunning eyes. Such a deep green flecked with gold and so very expressive. Secrets lay hidden there, secrets he wanted to discover. Sorrow, surely. Passion? He'd felt that and more when he'd kissed her in his mother's garden.

She was fierce, yet so small, a tempest in a teapot and a woman with a spirit he could only admire. The thought startled him. He wasn't in the habit of admiring women for more than their curves—though most assuredly, in that, this lass was truly blessed. He straightened, surprised to discover just how far he'd leaned across the counter.

The movement broke the spell.

Olivia snapped, "I fail to see why you are here. This matter is truly none of my concern. It's Deborah you should be speaking with. Not I. I would greatly appreciate you handling your own affairs."

Nicholas snorted. "I haven't spoken to Deborah in years, nor, might I add, was she the one to write. Why would I disturb the lass over a spiteful lie?"

"I do *not* lie," she retorted.

"Then, shall we pay Deborah a visit and settle this matter once and for all?" Nicholas crossed his arms as his irritation resurfaced. "We are but a short carriage ride away from the truth."

"I can scarcely pick up at the drop of a hat." She waved a hand at the shop.

He refrained from pointing out the lack of customers. "Then may I reserve the pleasure of your company tomorrow? Surely, you understand that I need your help. I can scarcely arrive at the Duke of Lennox's residence, unannounced, to discuss such a delicate matter."

She hesitated.

"Believe me, Miss Mackenzie, I have every intention of upholding the truth." He chuckled, then added, "If I am truly proven to be the father of your cousin's child, I will wed her within the week."

A flash of naked doubt crossed her face.

He grinned. So, she wasn't as believing of her cousin as she claimed.

The shop door rattled and opened. The bell rang, and a dark-haired man entered, his hat tucked under his arm, his gloves in hand, and a very finely carved, silver-handled walking stick hooked over his arm. Recognition punched Nicholas like a fist in the gut. Years. A good ten years had passed since he'd last seen Lord James Randall.

It wasn't long enough.

Lord Randall looked up, then froze, as if poised to flee.

Nicholas recovered first. "Fancy meeting you here, Randall," he grated through tightly clenched teeth.

Lord Randall closed the door behind him with a deliberate slowness, then answered, "So, my eyes do not deceive me. I didn't know you could be bothered to leave the card table, Blair."

The words sounded innocent and apt enough, given his reputation, but coming from Lord Randall's mouth, they took on quite a different meaning. Henrietta. Henrietta Kendrick, the woman who would always stand between them, the woman Nicholas had lost to Randall over his choice to play a game of cards that fateful night.

Nicholas drew a sharp breath. Even after ten years, the memory of Henrietta still hurt. His first love, lost, and long dead—thanks to the man standing before him.

"Do not allow me to interfere with your purchase, Randall," he clipped.

A calculating gleam sparked in Lord Randall's eyes. "Purchase? Perhaps, I've business of another sort, my dear fellow."

Nicholas tensed. There was no mistaking that look of smug satisfaction. Was the snake playing a game with Olivia? Like he'd bloody hell let *that* happen—not again.

"Nae." Nicholas lifted his mouth in a dangerous smile. "You will be leaving. Soon."

"Miss Mackenzie would have a say, I imagine," Lord Randall softly disagreed.

From the corner of his eye, Nicholas saw Olivia glance from man to man, clearly puzzled, but he couldn't let himself become distracted—not again.

"Nae," Nicholas replied, deadly calm. "You and your insidious ways are not welcome here."

Lord Randall's eye twitched. "Insidious? Simply because you lost?"

Lost? Did losing to a man who lied and bent the truth, truly count as a loss? While Nicholas had played his game, Randall had whispered lies into sweet Henrietta's so very innocent ears. He'd drowned her with glasses of wine. He'd broken her heart. Then, he'd invited himself into her bed. The next morning, she'd agreed to become the next Lady Randall. Her conscience had allowed her no other choice.

"You both fancy music, do you?" Olivia's voice broke the silence. "Piano arrangements? Violin? Perhaps both?" As they continued to glare at one another, she moved to the shelves and pulled out various sheets of music. "Might I recommend *The Soldier's Adieu*? A copy for each gentleman?"

Lord Randall's eyes narrowed at Nicholas. "I often find the past destined to repeat itself. Do you not agree?"

Nicholas snorted with contempt.

"*Robin Adair* and *Highland Hearth* are quite popular this year," Olivia said. "Might I also recommend the classics? Brahms? Mozart?"

Nicholas shot a glance at the lass. She was a far different creature than the retiring Henrietta. The thought comforted. He raised a brow at Lord Randall and warned in a low voice, "I will see you ruined if you try a single thing."

Lord Randall's nostrils flared.

Olivia returned to the counter, her arms overflowing. "No collection is complete without *The Lifework of Samuel Dunn*." She dropped the music into two stacks and slammed a palm down on each. "That's three crowns each, gentlemen."

Lord Randall blinked. Nicholas grinned. Nae, this feisty lass was a far cry from the shy Henrietta. If he were to bet, he'd wager his entire inheritance Lord Randall could never charm his way under Olivia's skirts.

"For such delightful service, I will gladly pay more." Nicholas chuckled and dropped a guinea on the counter.

Lord Randall hesitated.

"Surely, you wouldn't begrudge the lass her due?" Nicholas lifted a brow.

Lord Randall's face darkened. "I wager *you* are the one with creditors on your tail." He fished a handful of small coins from his pocket and slammed them down.

Nicholas eyed him, surprised at his response as well as the coins. Why would a man keep a pocketful of pennies?

"I thank you for your patronage, my lords." Olivia marched to the door and held it wide open. "Good day." She nodded her chin at the street.

Nicholas dropped his eyes over her fine figure. Damnation. Could a woman *be* more attractive? He picked up his music but took his time strolling toward the door, not only to ensure Lord Randall was truly leaving, but to prolong his enjoyment of the visual treat standing before him.

"Good day, my lord." Olivia curtsied as Lord Randall passed before her.

Randall touched the brim of his hat. "Good day, Miss Mackenzie."

Nicholas paused on the threshold, standing a little closer than politeness decreed.

"Good day, my lord." A wealth of emotion stormed in those green eyes.

Instinct informed him she was thinking of the kiss in the garden. His gaze dropped to her lips. He'd be tasting that sweetness again. He wouldn't stop until he did.

"Good day, Miss Mackenzie."

Then, with a gallant bow, he clapped his hat on his head and stepped into the street.

The door shut behind him. The next moment, he heard the click of the lock.

The corner of his lip lifted. She was a challenge, but he liked a good challenge right well enough. It only made victory all the sweeter.

CHAPTER 8

Olivia leaned against the door and heaved a sigh of relief. From the moment Nicholas had arrived, a whirlwind of intense emotions had stormed through her. Attraction, first. He'd stood so handsome in his tailored jacket, peering down at her with his cheek creased into a smile. His stunning blue eyes had drunk every inch of her. *Never* had her heart hammered more wildly.

Then, he'd spoken his name.

Anger and disappointment had swallowed her whole. But now? Dare she hope he'd spoken the truth? Dare she believe he hadn't fathered Deborah's child?

Had Deborah lied? Why?

She stepped to the window and peeked through the curtain just in time to catch a glimpse of Nicholas before he disappeared down the street. She understood the rumors now, the giggles behind the fans as the Season's debutants gossiped about Lady Blair's scandalously fascinating son. His lean buttocks and muscular thighs *did* draw the eye.

A foolish grin tugged her lips. Olivia stepped back with a snort. She had better things to do than ogle someone through a curtain, drooling like a madwoman—especially over the man who had fathered a child with her cousin.

She returned to the counter and swept the coins scattered there into a pile. One caught on her fingers. A bent shilling. Strange. She already had one of those. Well, now she had two. She dropped the entire lot safely into her pocket, then turned her steps back to the print room.

Many proclaimed the work of setting the type to be tedious, a true bore—but not her. She found the task relaxing, and when she was done, she quite enjoyed running her fingers over the fine lead engravings, pleased that not even the smallest casting stood out of line.

Today, however, there was nothing soothing to setting the rows. Her thoughts whirled between Nicholas's arrival, to his kiss in the garden, and then back again.

Setting the type took twice longer than usual, and when she finally finished, the late afternoon skies had darkened with rain. Big, fat drops.

Olivia twisted her lip in a grimace and hurried up the stairs at the back of the shop to her room above. The ping of water striking the pans met her ears as she opened her bedroom door. She already had four pots placed strategically beneath the leaks. From the puddle forming on the floorboards at the foot of her small bed, it was time to add another pot to the collection. She hurried back down the stairs.

Mrs. Lambert met her in the kitchen. "You will run out of pots, lass."

Olivia shot her a rueful grin. "I will fix the roof in the morning. It's too dark, now."

"That's men's work." Mrs. Lambert sniffed. The hairs sprouting from her mole bobbed in agreement.

Olivia shrugged. "I have no coin for a roofer." She nodded at the clay tiles stacked in the corner of the kitchen. "Besides, I have three tiles left from last time. Surely, replacing them can't be that hard. No doubt, it will just take me twice as long. I'll just start at dawn." With luck, she'd be finished in time to open the shop at the usual hour.

Mrs. Lambert lifted a doubtful brow. "Then, you'll need me earlier?"

"Please." Olivia smiled, fished out Lord Randall's small coins from her apron pocket, and gave Mrs. Lambert her pay.

By the time she'd seen the woman to the door and her father safely in bed, the rain began to fall in earnest. Smothering a yawn, she dropped a small iron pot at the foot of the bed and shrugged into her nightdress amidst the various pings and plops of the drops hitting the pots and pans.

Exhausted, she burrowed under the patched quilt and against the symphony of sound, let sleep carry her away. Strangely, her last conscience thought was the memory of Nicholas's lips on hers.

Olivia woke with a start. Judging by the warmth of the sun on her face, she'd overslept. She raised herself on her elbows. The view outside the window revealed a patchy sky. She surveyed the mismatched collection of cookery ware dotting her floor. A new leak had sprouted during the night.

She threw her covers back with a huff. She had time enough to fix at least one roof tile—she was running out of pots and pans.

She slipped off her nightdress and into a pair of her father's breeches, along with one of his gray linen shirts and, tying her hair back from her face, jogged down the narrow stairs.

The welcoming aroma of eggs and bacon guided her to the kitchen. "Good morning, Mrs. Lambert."

"Good morning, lass." The woman didn't acknowledge her breeches. Mrs. Lambert understood the necessity of Olivia wearing men's clothing, for operating the press and for other tasks about the house, but she still pretended she didn't see.

Olivia smiled and joined her father as he sat at the table, his eyes locked unseeing out the window. "Good morning, father," she murmured, and dropped a kiss on the top of his head.

He didn't move. Not that she expected him to. He never responded to her this early in the day. He stayed within his silent shell until Mrs. Lambert guided him to his piano.

"Take this, lass." Mrs. Lambert pressed a thick slice of bacon wrapped in a bannock into her hands, still refusing to look at her breeches.

Olivia chuckled and stepped out into the fresh morning air. The rain from the night before made everything appear clean and bright. She ate quickly, dusted her hands on the back of her breeches, then dragged the ladder from the back of the small fenced yard to prop against the side of the townhouse.

The clay tile weighed more than she liked and balancing it on her shoulder while ascending the ladder was far harder than it had looked when she'd watched the roofer before. Still, while it was very slow going, she finally succeeded in shoving the tile onto the lip of the roof and glanced around.

She groaned. From the looks of the roof, there were at least five more broken tiles—maybe more. With a scowl, she descended, grabbed the hammer from the print room, then returned to the roof to knock the first cracked tile free. Her arms had already begun to ache when she pulled out the last broken piece and kicked it off the roof. She paused and wiped sweat from her forehead. She was fortunate, truly, that her roof wasn't a steep one, but even so, she slipped more than once as she dragged the new tile into place.

By the time she'd finally finished settling the tile into place, sweat dripped from her brow and stained the back of her shirt. One tile. *One damnable, infernal tile.* She'd spent the entire morning on the thing, and from her newfound perch, she could see at least a dozen more that needed replacing.

"Damn it all to hell," she swore under her breath. She wasn't usually one to swear, but if ever a situation required it, this one certainly did.

She swung her leg over the roof's edge, located the ladder rung with her foot, and began to climb down. A few feet from the ground, hands startled her from behind, locking themselves nearly under her arms onto the ladder rails. She gasped in surprise and fell back against a man's hard chest.

"My apologies," Nicholas rumbled in her ear. "I didn't mean to startle you."

Against her will, her heart pounded with excitement even as her temper flared. She whirled as his hands slipped around her waist, effectively caging her in his arms.

"I could have broken my neck," she snapped.

"Hardly." He grinned. "Not when I am right here." He lowered his lashes, strangely thick dark ones even though his hair was blond.

She frowned in an effort to clear her thoughts and added acidly, "Or sprained my ankle."

"You were on the last rung," he murmured, his lips still quirked upwards in amusement. "And may I point out, I *did* catch you."

He pulled her closer as if to underscore the declaration. She felt the heat of his hard chest, mere inches from her breasts. Her heart leapt into her throat, and for the briefest of moments, she wanted him to kiss her again.

Then, sanity returned. This man soon would—or should—wed her cousin.

Gathering her brows into a frown, she broke from his grasp.

"Women should wear breeches more often," he murmured as she stepped away.

Startled, she glanced up. "That's a scandalous thing to say," she retorted in an effort to ignore her racing pulse.

"Why?" he asked with a lazy lift of a brow. "The garment befits them quite admirably, I must say. Surely, there is nothing wrong with admiring the female form?"

He had a way with words that thrilled the blood. Determined to ignore him, she asked bluntly, "Why are you here?"

He answered easily enough. "Why, I came to fetch you, my dear. Are we not calling upon your cousin? My carriage awaits."

If he thought she was going anywhere in a carriage with him, he was so very sadly mistaken. "I do not recall agreeing to such a thing." She pursed her lips and pointed to the roof. "Even if I had, I have a roof to repair."

Nicholas cast an eye at the roof, then arched an amused brow. "I will send for a roofer."

"I cannot afford one." Olivia took a step toward the kitchen for another tile.

He caught her quickly by the wrist. She held still. His fingers felt like fire.

"Did I ask you to pay?" he drawled.

Olivia shook her hand free. "It's my roof that needs fixing."

This time, he stepped forward, easily blocking her way and she was forced to look into his face. The expression in his eyes made her heart skip a beat, the expression of a man not even bothering to hide his interest. What had he said? *Aye, a true man doesn't let the lass that caught his interest slip through his fingers. He goes after her.*

But then, it was such a very rakish thing to say.

Suddenly, Mrs. Lambert's head popped out the back door, "Oliva, darling, there's a man to see you in the shop."

From her dour expression, it was clearly a man Olivia didn't wish to see. "Who, Mrs. Lambert?"

"I wouldn't know, lass," the woman replied. "But he smells of the banking sort."

Olivia frowned, murmured a distracted, "If you'll excuse me," then ran through the back door and up the stairs. In less than three minutes, she'd changed into a dress and dragged a comb through her hair and dashed back down the stairs.

On the last step, she drew a deep breath and, adopting a sedate pace, headed for the front shop. Pausing behind the curtains, she peeked through the opening.

"Damnation," she swore under her breath.

It was Mr. Pitt, the owner of the Theater Royale, standing by the counter with his pudgy fingers laced behind his back and his bald spot prominently on display—despite the straggly tufts of hair he'd combed sideways to hide his loss of hair.

Her mouth went dry. What brought him here? Her last payment wasn't due for a few more weeks.

"Good morning, Mr. Pitt," she forced a measure of warmth in her voice as she entered the room. "How pleasant to see you. How might I be of service?"

The man turned and gave a curt nod that sufficed as a greeting. "This letter." He pulled a letter from his waistcoat. With a flick of his wrist, he slid the paper across the counter. "'Tis a might concerning, it is. Read it, right quick."

Wordlessly, Olivia picked up the letter and began to read.

DEAR MR. PITT,

I am writing to inform you that I will no longer be singing An Enchanted Summer Evening…

OLIVIA'S HEART STOOD STILL. SHE GRIPPED THE LETTER TIGHTLY, unable to read anything more, other than the name scrawled at the bottom: Louisa.

"As you very well know, Miss Mackenzie," Mr. Pitt's voice droned in the background, "I foresaw this exact risk when I agreed to rent the Theatre Royale for this concert. Our contract states that all monies are due, in the event I deem it necessary to collect them—which I do so, now. Fetch the coin and right quick." He paused, then his voice altered when he continued, "Unless, of course, you seek alternative arrangements—"

Olivia crushed the letter in her hand. "She will sing. I have contracts myself, Mr. Pitt. She will sing."

He stared at her, eyes cold. "Then show me these contracts, along with the remainder due. Otherwise, I will not hold the date."

The remainder? She only had eighteen pounds in her keeping, not the twenty owed. Why was he being so obstinate? He couldn't have a host of performers eager to perform in the summer months, but she knew better than to challenge the man.

"The remainder," he repeated, his voice low. He didn't mention 'alternate payments' again—verbally, anyway. He let the lift of his eyebrow and the quick glance at her breasts speak, instead.

"Very well," she snapped. "I will show you the contracts."

Olivia marched through the curtains, her mind racing. She was short two pounds. Perhaps seeing the contracts would be enough? Would he accept something as a good faith gesture? She couldn't bear to part with her mother's locket, but did she have something else of value the man might accept? Nae.

Tears gathered at the thought of handing over her mother's locket. But the payment was only half the problem. Louisa. She scowled. Well, she'd show the woman the contract. She'd *force* her to sing if there was no other recourse. Such an action would end their friendship—but then, it didn't matter, not when they weren't much of friends to begin with.

If only she could find someone else to sing, but it was too late. There wasn't enough time, and of all the opera singers she knew, only Louisa could draw a large enough crowd.

She closed the print room door behind her and dropped to her knees before the secret floorboard. Again, tears burned her lashes at the thought of giving the odious man her mother's locket, but what choice did she truly have? What could she possibly say to convince him to wait? At a loss, she pried the floorboard loose and pulled out the box. It was unusually light. Puzzled, she lifted the lid.

Her heart stood still.

The box was empty.

Frantically, she searched the cavity in the floor. There was nothing there. Her coins, the contracts, and her mother's locket...*gone*.

"Nae," she gasped. "Nae. Nae. *Nae*."

Panic seized her. Who could have taken her things? William? Mrs. Lambert? They were the only two in the house besides her father. Mrs. Lambert wouldn't. She was practically family, and in her heart, she knew William wouldn't, as well. He was a simple lad, incapable of such things. Biting back the tears, she jumped to her feet and ran to the parlor. Nicholas sat in the chair opposite Mrs. Lambert, listening to her father play the piano.

"What is it, child?" Mrs. Lambert rose to her feet, alarmed.

"The box," Olivia choked. "The box in the print room."

"Box?"

The genuine confusion on the old woman's brow made Olivia feel guilty for even mentioning the matter. She drew a shaky breath. "William? Have you seen him?" She hadn't let him go yet. Perhaps, he'd stumbled on the box by accident and thought it a lost treasure, free for the taking?

"William's snoring in the kitchen, lass."

She was off to the kitchen before Mrs. Lambert had finished the sentence.

"The box, William," Olivia gasped as she shook him awake. "Where is the box?"

"Box?" William mumbled, looking even more puzzled than Mrs. Lambert had.

The tears flowed then. With a sob, Olivia sank to her knees. She was ruined. It made little difference if Louisa sang now. The man would cancel the venue. Without the concert, she would be forced to sell the printing press...and without the press, how would she and her father survive?

She remained on her knees, the tears sliding down her cheeks. Slowly, she forced herself to breathe. Sniveling never solved a thing. Not once had tears provided much needed help. An image of her grandfather snaked through her mind—not the image of a friendly source of strength, of aid, but a tall, stern man who would no doubt be delighted to see her fail.

She gritted her teeth. She wasn't giving up. Nae, she would give him not a single jot of satisfaction. She would see her father's songs sung in the Theater Royale and she would sell every blasted book of music she'd ever printed—with or without Louisa's help. Aye, she would hire someone to find Louisa. She'd force her to sing, with or without the contract. The woman was greedy. Surely, she couldn't refuse a doubling of her fee?

Right now, she had to convince Mr. Pitt to wait without having to sell her soul—but then, it wasn't her soul that he wanted. She shoved to her feet, wiped her eyes, and straightened her hair.

"Mr. Pitt," she began as she stepped through the curtains.

Nicholas glanced up from the counter, where he flipped through the pages of *Delightful Summer Songs of the Heart*. "I am afraid Mr. Pitt has been called away on urgent business," he said with a circumspect nod. "He asked me to convey the message that he would return on the original agreed upon date for the last payment."

Olivia blinked. She glanced around the room, unable to believe his words. "Surely, you misunderstood."

"Ah, here." Nicholas fished in his waistcoat pocket and pulled out a piece of paper. It was Louisa's crumpled letter, but there was new writing on the back. "He did remember to write it down. Signed it, as well, I believe."

Olivia read the spidery scrawl on the back. Indeed, it was Mr. Pitt's recognizable script, though somewhat shakier than usual.

"Why?" she wondered, aloud.

Nicholas yawned. "I couldn't say."

Olivia cocked a brow and looked him in the eye. He met her gaze easily enough, the corners of his chiseled lips quirking at the edges.

Then, the sight of Louisa's name rekindled her anger. "You have a carriage, do you not, Lord Blair?"

"Indeed, I do."

"Then I must impose upon you. I need a ride to Number Fourteen, Parsonage Square. As payment, I will willingly assist with your business with my cousin."

His blue eyes gleamed as he executed an elaborate bow. "I am at your service, Miss Mackenzie."

CHAPTER 9

NICHOLAS EYED THE LASS SEATED ACROSS THE CARRIAGE, SWAYING from side to side as the carriage navigated the potholes in the road. The sight of her weeping on the kitchen floor had disturbed him, deeply. He hadn't meant to eavesdrop, but as the events played out, he was glad he had.

Mr. Pitt had been easy to browbeat. Within minutes, he'd agreed to honor his original contract, his hand had shaken so strongly, he'd nearly broken the quill when he'd written the message. He scarcely finished before he'd run out the door.

Nicholas suppressed a chuckle and glanced out the window. In the past, he would have used the situation to seduce the object of his desire into his bed. Strangely, this time, he wished his help to remain unknown.

The carriage turned onto Parsonage Square, a pleasant enough street with rows of townhouses bordering a park dotted with bluebells. At the fourth townhouse from the end of the row, the carriage stopped.

With a pleasant smile, Nicholas exited the carriage and offered his hand. "Allow me, Miss Mackenzie."

She spared him a curt glance, her mind clearly on her

predicament.

"Shall I wait in the carriage?" he asked as she joined him on the street.

"Please do," she muttered. "I cannot imagine I'll be long."

He tipped his hat as she marched past him to the door. Then, he lounged against his carriage and crossed his arms, he watched her rounded derriere from under hooded eyes.

The third time Olivia rapped the heavy brass knocker, a heavyset maid answered the door. She squinted at the carriage before asking Olivia, "How may I help you, Miss?" Her sour voice easily carried to Nicholas's ears.

"I must speak with Miss Hamilton, at once, please." Olivia handed the woman her card.

The maid gave it a glance, then shook her head. "I am sorry, Miss Mackenzie, but Miss Hamilton went off last night. She didn't tell us where."

Olivia's spine visibly straightened.

With another nod, the maid closed the door.

Slowly, Olivia turned and swept back to the carriage, her head held high and her jaw set with determination. By God, she was a fighter. Her fingers rested small in his hand and her touch light as he handed her back inside the carriage.

"Where to?" he asked.

"The duke's townhouse, is it not?" she asked with a distant smile. "I am a woman of my word."

She settled into her seat and smoothed her skirts over her knees as flashes of anger crossed her face, but by the time they exited Parsonage Square, she abandoned all semblance of control.

"The harridan," she seethed. "The *strumpet*." Her nostrils flared.

Nicholas eyed her in admiration. He'd always been attracted to bold women with spirit. "I take it that Miss Hamilton has betrayed you?"

"Indeed, betrayal seems to be the theme of the month." Olivia lifted her chin.

By God, she was a voluptuous goddess of temptation. "Yet, you're not one to wilt into vapors."

She snorted in dry amusement. "If wilting solved the matter, my lord, I would be the first on the floor."

He chuckled. "With your spirit, I have no doubt you will succeed in your endeavors, Miss Mackenzie." Indeed, she'd win through sheer strength of will alone. "If I can be of service, please let me know."

She met his gaze squarely. "Tempting, to be sure," she murmured.

"Tempting?" he queried, intrigued.

"Louisa has a weakness for charming men," she answered, as if thinking aloud.

"You find me charming?" He arched an amused brow.

"You have quite the reputation, do you not?" Her voice held a mocking note.

His mirth faded. "Perhaps, but I am a changed man." Of late, he seemed to be changing by the day.

Silence fell, a strangely peaceful one, despite the situation, and one in which he felt no need for unnecessary conversation. Instead, he observed Olivia from under his brows as she stared at Glasgow's streets. He'd thought her bonny from the start, but the more she resisted and ignored him, his fascination grew, and by the time they arrived at the Duke of Lennox's townhouse, he found himself hooked like a fish.

THE MOMENT NICHOLAS LAID EYES ON DEBORAH, PITY STIRRED, and his irritation melted away. The lass looked downright terrible. Dark circles ringed her eyes, a gray pallor tinged her skin, and her hair hung in limp brown ringlets.

"Lord Blair," she whispered hoarsely, her eyes darting nervously to Olivia and back again.

Nicholas bowed his most courteous bow.

Deborah took one look and rushed to Olivia's side. "Why… why?" she hissed, grabbing Olivia's hands, a fine sheen of sweat beading her brow. "*Why is he here?*"

Did the lass truly think he couldn't hear?

"Lord Blair's come to make things right, Deborah," Olivia assured with a sympathetic smile.

"Olivia," Deborah gasped, and stumbled to the settee. "*Olivia*, what did you tell him? Olivia?" Horror and despair warred in her voice.

"Why, I told him what…he needed to know." Clearly, Olivia was puzzled.

Her cousin buried her face in her hands. "No. No," she gasped. "Not him. He shouldn't be here. *Olivia, what did you do?*"

Perplexed, Olivia gingerly sat by her side. "There's no cause to fret, Deborah. Whatever do you mean?"

"What is this?"

Nicholas looked up to see the Duke of Lennox standing in the doorway, wearing a dark green kilt, his thick brows drawn in a stern line.

"Please," Deborah sobbed. "*Let me faint.*"

Nicholas straightened but before he could take action, Olivia rose.

"It appears I have unnecessarily upset my cousin." She faced her grandfather.

The man scowled. "She's ever prone to fits of vapors." He turned to Nicholas. "Lord Blair, why are you here?"

The eyes of both women latched onto him, at once, Olivia's keen and alert, with Deborah's growing rounder by the second. Indeed, it was a miracle she hadn't fainted already.

Nicholas dipped in an easy bow. "Good day, Your Grace. It is my pleasure to escort Miss Mackenzie about her business this day, and as I have been remiss in paying my respects to Lady Deborah these past two years, I merely sought to use the occasion to make amends."

The duke tossed him a cynical look, then cocked a grizzled brow at Olivia. "Explain yourself."

She lifted her chin and met him with a cool, confident gaze. "What is to explain? Am I not free to appreciate the company of my cousin?"

"Then you find hysteria particularly enjoyable?" The duke crossed his arms, his expression peeved.

Deborah whimpered like a lost puppy.

"Indeed, I much prefer hysteria to cruelty," Oliva replied with a pointed stare.

The duke's brows snaked higher. "Dare you accuse me of cruelty, insolent girl?"

"I merely stated my preferences, did I not?" Olivia challenged in turn, then turned back to her cousin. "My dear Deborah. I must be going."

Her cousin jumped to her feet and grabbed Olivia's hands. "You will return?"

"Of course. There's no need to fret," Olivia promised, and kissed Deborah's cheek before turning back to the duke who still stood in the doorway. "I will be leaving now."

Boldly, she strode to the door, seeming as if she'd walk right over the man. At the last moment, he stepped aside and stared, as if she'd sprouted horns as she swept down the stairs. Nicholas suppressed a chuckle. The woman had spirit. A jolt of excited pleasure rocked through him. This was a woman he simply had to bed.

Suddenly aware of the duke's penetrating gaze locked upon him, he turned toward Deborah and bowed his farewell. "Perhaps, I shall have the honor of your company soon, my lady?"

The lass responded with a kind of muffled squeak that provoked a momentary concern for her health, but after assuring himself she still breathed, he turned and faced the duke.

The man's gaze had apparently never strayed. Somewhat unsettled, Nicholas cleared his throat. "Your Grace—"

"What business do you have with my granddaughter?" the man interrupted harshly.

Nicholas cast an uneasy brow at Deborah.

"Not that one," the duke snapped, impatience threading his voice. He nodded at the stairs. "Olivia."

Ah, so the duke's cantankerousness masked a decided interest in the lass, did it? Nicholas tilted his head. "I—"

"I am aware of your reputation, Lord Blair," the duke cut him short. He furrowed his brows and glared for a good ten seconds before grunting, "Have a care."

Deborah squeaked again, but the duke scarcely noticed.

"Most certainly, Your Grace," Nicholas assured. He cleared his throat again, strangely a little ill at ease.

After a moment, the duke nodded. Once. "You may go."

With one last dip of his chin vaguely in Deborah's direction, Nicholas left. He caught up with Olivia as she waited on the townhouse step.

"Allow me to send for my carriage—" he began.

She whirled, her auburn curls bouncing in irritation along with the rest of her. "Oh, I have already taken care of that," she replied, her jaw tight. "The *audacity* of the man."

There was no doubt of whom she spoke. Few stood up to the Duke of Lennox—he'd ruined more than one man with a single word. Yet, this wee lass hadn't hesitated to challenge him.

A sizzle of attraction raced down the back of his neck. He let his gaze trail slowly over her curves as his coach-and-four rolled to a stop before them in a jingle of horses' harnesses.

Olivia barely acknowledged him as he handed her inside the carriage, and as they started to roll, he couldn't help but notice the manner of her scowl. She sat on the seat opposite him, her brows drawn in an expression very much like her grandfather's. They were strikingly similar, now that he'd seen them side by side. Obviously, he couldn't tell her. She'd doubtlessly behead him. He suppressed a smile and lounged back in his seat as she glared out the window at Glasgow's passing streets, every line in her slender form rigid.

There was much to concern her, of course. Clearly, Deborah had landed herself in a fine fettle, but her surprised reaction to his presence surely had planted a seed of doubt in Olivia's mind? But then, the female mind was truly a mystery.

In what seemed like mere minutes, his coach stopped before Olivia's door and again, he was handing her out.

"Miss Mackenzie—" he began as her hand touched his.

"I must help her," she interrupted with a frown.

Damnation, but couldn't the lass see just how like her grandfather she truly was? Neither had little compunction over interrupting as it pleased them.

"No doubt, your cousin is in a situation," Nicholas granted. "And though it is clearly not one of my making, I do wish to assist, as I may."

Olivia's frown deepened. "I have yet to hear her explanation, my lord. I will arrange a better time and place. Good day."

With that, she whirled and made for her door. His irritation at being so quickly dismissed faded at the sight of her hips swaying from side to side. By George, those hips could tempt a man. A sudden heat rushed to his loins.

There was only one way forward on this matter if he wanted Olivia in his bed.

He had to solve her cousin's dilemma, first, and for that, he needed the truth. If the man who fathered her child was marriageable, he would play the role of negotiator.

If he wasn't, he'd find one that was...and then? He did chuckle aloud. Then, he would make Olivia his.

CHAPTER 10

A RAINDROP STRUCK THE TIP OF OLIVIA'S NOSE AS SHE REACHED for the knob of the shop's door. She shot a quick glance at the dark clouds overhead as a gust of wind blasted her face. No doubt, it would be another night for the pots.

The day had been a horrible one in all respects. She'd lost every penny she'd saved. While, with hard work, she could recover, it was still a terrible blow. And Nicholas? From the moment he'd arrived, her pulse hadn't stopped racing. What kind of woman was she? She couldn't harbor feelings for her cousin's soon-to-be husband...but then, Deborah hadn't responded as expected on that score. She'd acted as if she hadn't wanted Nicholas there.

She must visit Deborah, soon— when their grandfather wasn't there—to clear the confusion. Olivia clenched her jaw. Her grandfather. Nae. She wouldn't waste a single moment of her time thinking of that cantankerous old man—especially when she had a roof to fix and a concert to organize.

With her thoughts in circles, she hurried to the parlor.

"Good evening, child," Mrs. Lambert greeted as Olivia stepped inside. "I am afraid it's bad news. The night watchman's been down with a fever this past week, and the neighbors have noticed naught a thing."

Olivia grimaced. Of course, such would be her luck. Her money was as good as gone. She didn't even want to think of her mother's locket.

"Still, you mustn't give up hope," Mrs. Lambert said. She tilted her head at the window. The rain had begun to fall in earnest. "It's not all bad news. 'Tis raining something dreadful."

"That isn't bad because?" Olivia scowled. Her shoulders ached. She couldn't bear the thought of lugging even more tiles onto the roof.

To her surprise, Mrs. Lambert chuckled. "Then, you haven't noticed."

Olivia glanced around the tiny room. Nothing had changed. Her father still sat at the piano, locked in his own world. Puzzled, she turned back to the woman. "Noticed?"

"I shan't spoil the surprise then, lass."

Olivia shook her head, bewildered, but when no more information was forthcoming, she shrugged and joined her father at the piano. This night, he didn't respond when she dropped a kiss on the top of his head. He stared into the distance, his fingers running over the keys. The melody was a sad one. Mournful. Tears misted her eyes. She knew what it meant. His thoughts dwelt upon her mother.

Olivia turned away.

"You will need me in the morning, lass?" Mrs. Lambert asked gently.

"Early, if you can." Olivia dug in her reticule for the shillings and dropped them in the old woman's hand. At least, she could still pay that small debt. She yawned and cocked a rueful brow at the steady beat of the rain outside. "I still have a roof to repair." Then, music to print and deliver, musicians to pay... and an opera singer to find. She sighed. "Is William still here?"

Mrs. Lambert hefted herself from her chair and began

packing her darning into her basket. "His mum came and fetched the lad. His da's gone and broke his leg on the farm. He's needed at home, child."

Olivia frowned, frustrated, although she couldn't deny a sense of relief. As far as shop boys went, he did precious little for his pay. Most likely, he'd saved her the trouble of letting him go.

"You will be a sight faster without him, lass," Mrs. Lambert commented with a nod, her mole hairs bobbing in agreement. "Well then, I'll be off."

As the door closed behind her, Olivia led her father past the kitchen to his bedroom on the other side. At the door, she paused and breathed deeply of the faint rose and lavender scent. Even after nearly four years, the room still smelled like her mother. It was almost as if the curtains, counterpane and rug didn't want to let her go as much as they didn't.

With a sigh, she guided her father to the bed. He sank against his pillow and expelled a long breath himself, but then, for the briefest of moments, a lucid gleam entered his eye.

"You need to oil the Devil's Tail, lass. I can hear it squeaking all the way into the parlor."

Olivia blinked. She'd noticed the sound from the printing press's handle just that morning.

"And check the tympan alignment. There's a knocking that's worrisome."

Olivia held her breath. Knowing she had only a fleeting moment, she looked deeply into her father's eyes. "I love you, Father." Before she'd even finished, he was already fading away.

"Olivia, child, my how you've grown," he murmured absently.

His moments of clarity were so few and far between, mostly serving as a painful reminder of what she'd lost. Sometimes, she wondered if she'd rather not have them, at all.

Tears robbed her of speech. She was grateful for the wind,

rattling the shutters and driving the rain against the slats. It was loud, like the pattering of thousands of tiny feet. She waited for the rain to subside, and then composure regained, squeezed her father's hand.

"Good night, Father."

"Good night, my child."

He was asleep before she left his room.

She paused to inspect the kitchen shutters. She'd have to replace them soon. The hinges had nearly rusted through. Olivia expelled a long breath. The townhouse was falling down around her. She scowled. Why did everything require so much money to repair? Shoving the worries of the day aside, she tiredly padded up the stairs to her tiny room and with a sigh, quickly undressed and slipped into bed.

Ten minutes passed before she finally noticed.

The rain still drummed against the windows, rattling the shutters and pinging on the cobblestones, but the pots in her room were oddly silent.

Curious, she rose from bed and held out her palms.

Nothing.

Her roof had been repaired.

"Paid," the roofer, Mr. Tisdale, said.

"Paid?" Olivia asked for the third time, still unable to believe her ears.

"His lordship paid for the entire roof. Now, if you have opinions, you will have to speak with Lord Blair, Miss Mackenzie. I have work to do." The wizened man nodded firmly, his patience at an end. He always reminded Olivia of an elvish sprite, slight, spry and with twinkling blue eyes, yet the fingers he lifted to the corners of his mouth were calloused from years of hard work. He let out a shrill whistle.

Three heads poked over the rim of the roof above.

"Aye?" three voices chorused.

"Step down, lads. The tiles have arrived." Mr. Tisdale nodded his pointed chin toward the front of the townhouse, then turned back to Olivia. "Now, if you will kindly stay out of the way. I am not one to have womenfolk underfoot. These stone tiles can be dangerous. Wouldn't do to have you hurt, now."

Olivia suppressed a snort from her perch on the back stoop. She could hardly harass the man simply because Nicholas had decided to barge into her affairs.

"Very well, then," she muttered, and closed the door behind her with a bang.

"What a surprise." Mrs. Lambert looked up from the kitchen stove. "And a nice one, after…"

Olivia scowled, hardly needing a reminder of the theft. Would the problems never end? Nicholas had no business paying for her roof—especially an entirely new one. Of course, a man of his wealth wouldn't understand the hardship she'd incur in repaying him. Lord knew, she couldn't afford even a handful of tiles with the contents of her box lost.

"Are you sucking on a lemon, lass?" Mrs. Lambert chuckled.

Olivia shot her a sour look and reached for her gloves draped on the back of a kitchen chair. "I cannot accept such charity, but I have Lady Winthrop's event to attend. Perhaps, Lord Blair will be there."

"Best of luck to you. I will mind the shop while you're gone."

Olivia smiled her thanks and swept down the narrow hall.

She could only spare Nicholas so much thought. If he *was* at Lady Winthrop's, she'd take up the roof matter, at once. If he wasn't…well…even though she hadn't a clue where he was staying, no doubt, he would show up soon enough as Deborah's plight was, as yet, still unresolved.

Right now, she had far more pressing matters. She had to find Louisa. Desperately. The aspiring young soprano, Elena Goodman, had contracted to sing *Softly, My Heart* at Lady Winthrop's charity event. Perhaps she knew of Louisa's whereabouts. They were, after all, the closest of friends.

Olivia collected her hat from the shop counter and left the shop. The day was bright; all traces of last night's storm had vanished. A pleasant breeze played with the ends of her long hat ribbons as she hurried down the cobblestone street, nodding greetings to each passerby.

Gaily dressed folk strolled the paths of Glasgow Green as she entered the park. She'd gone no more than ten yards before she spied Mr. Pitt with his wife on his arm. Olivia altered course at once, but spared a quick glance at the dowdy woman at his side. As usual, she walked with her chin high, but with a perpetual look of disappointment on her face—but then, with Mr. Pitt as a husband, such feelings were entirely understandable.

"Move along, Mrs. Pitt," Mr. Pitt said, his voice carrying across the green. "Move along, right quick."

Olivia rolled her eyes and hurried down the woodland path. Lady Winthrop's house wasn't far, just down the lane that bordered the eastern side of Glasgow Green, overlooking the river. Though newly built, the tidy establishment still held an older-world charm with its arched doorways, diamond-paned windows, and rough-hewn beams.

Carriages lined the drive, horses stamped lazily in their harnesses under the tall, nearby oaks. The coachmen laughed and played a game of battledore and shuttlecock. They waved as Olivia passed and ducked inside the servant's entrance at the back of the house.

"Lawks, there you are, Miss Mackenzie."

It was Elena. The young brunette hovered by the door,

plucking the feathers sewn on her dress, her soft, brown eyes worried.

Relief flooded through Olivia. "I am so pleased you're here. We need to speak—"

Elena grimaced and grabbed her arm, pulling her close. "That's just it, Olivia," she whispered. "I shouldn't be here, at all. Louisa will be furious."

Anger flashed over Olivia. "Do you know where she is?"

The young singer shook her head and glanced away, looking almost guilty.

So, she *did* know. "Please, tell me. I must speak with her."

"She's not going to sing for your concert, Olivia. Not anymore," Elena whispered.

"But, but I have *contracts*." Or, she *had*, but Elena didn't need to know that.

Elena hesitated, then confessed in a rush, "I cannot sing for you anymore, either, Olivia. I feel so very dreadful over the matter, but she'll ruin me and she has *connections*. I had to tell Lady Winthrop I suffer from a sore throat. I brought Marie. She's in the drawing room, now."

Olivia blinked. Another betrayal? And Marie? Marie Geertz. She worked closely with Foster and Sons' Publishing House. They specialized in the classics, not the lighthearted ditties that she printed.

"I am sorry," Elena choked. "I really am."

Olivia sucked a deep breath. "But you signed a contract yourself—"

"I cannot. I really cannot." Elena blanched, then pushed past Olivia to run out of the house.

Olivia closed her eyes, battling the sudden urge to bang her forehead against the wall.

Why bother with contracts? The singers treated them like discarded letters from a scorned lover. But then, perhaps they knew she didn't have them any longer. She drew a sharp breath. Had Louisa had a hand in the robbery? Stolen her mother's locket?

The sounds of Mozart's *"O zittre nicht, mein lieber Sohn"* drifted from the floor above, intruding upon her thoughts. Of course, it was music she never printed.

She left the house. Lady Winthrop wouldn't miss her. The women of society tolerated her presence at their charity gatherings out of pity and respect to Lady Blair. Blowing her hair out of her face, she headed for a row of willows that bordered the banks of the River Clyde. The wind rustled the long, sweeping branches as she walked through them.

She needed a new plan. She still owed Mr. Pitt fifteen pounds and another five for the musicians. The concert was in a month. She had a month to convince Louisa to return or she really *would* be out on the streets, as a true charity case of her own.

Olivia closed her eyes and rubbed the back of her neck. Was this really over a man? And of all men...Lord Randall? Something about him made her hackles rise. He spoke so smoothly and in far too polished a manner—almost as if he had something to hide.

"Miss Mackenzie."

Olivia jerked and glanced over her shoulder. There he was, as if summoned by her thoughts. The man himself: Lord Randall. He stood just a few yards away, elegantly dressed in tanned breeches, fine polished black leather boots and black velvet top hat.

"Are you avoiding me, Miss Mackenzie?" he teased.

Did wishing to avoid him *now* count? Olivia forced herself to smile—he was a customer, after all. "Nae, my lord."

"Every time I visit the shop, I find you're not there," he explained, even though she hadn't asked.

He'd been coming to the shop? Why did she find that

disturbing? "How can I help you, my lord? Are you looking for something in particular?"

He smiled, an easy smile, and one obviously of the flirtatious kind. "Perhaps, I did not visit for the music."

Olivia took an unwitting step back. The slight muscle twitch on his jaw informed her he'd noticed.

"Miss Mackenzie," a new voice hailed her from behind.

Nicholas ducked under the trailing branches to join her and looking handsomer than ever in his gray breeches and a dark silk cravat, intricately tied.

"Randall." His tone announced it was scarcely a greeting.

"Blair," Lord Randall acknowledged through clenched teeth.

The two men stared at each in grim distaste. Clearly, something stood between them, but that was no business of hers. She had pressing matters of her own.

Olivia cleared her throat. "If you will excuse me, gentlemen? I must be going."

Nicholas's eyes shifted to hers, at once. "My carriage awaits."

"Allow me, Miss Mackenzie," Lord Randall said at the same time.

"I can walk on my own, thank you." She stepped through the willow branches.

Nicholas caught up with her before she got halfway across the lawn. "I shall accompany you, Olivia."

She didn't need to turn around to know Lord Randall watched her by the willows. She felt his eyes boring through the back of her head.

"Shall we?" Nicholas offered his arm.

She should have merely thanked him, of course, and then promptly left, alone, but then, he looped her arm through his. The muscles resting beneath her fingertips were stone hard, warm, and imbued with the power to sweep all other thoughts away—even the most worrisome ones. A flush of warmth snaked down her spine as they left the grounds, heading back to Glasgow Green.

At the edge of the park, she regained her presence of mind. "Thank you, but truly, I have no need for an escort."

"I quite disagree."

He towered over her. She'd known he was tall, of course, but now, he seemed doubly so. She frowned at her beating heart and schooled her thoughts. He was meant for her cousin. He belonged to Deborah. As much as she found it depressing, it was time to distance herself, set boundaries.

"I understand." She adopted a formal tone. "Soon, we will be family, will we not? As my cousin, you will—"

"That's utter tripe," he interrupted with a snort.

"I beg your pardon?"

He stopped in his tracks and peered down at her, looking rather irritated. "You know very well I am not the father of her child."

Oh, how she didn't want him to be. Desire flared. She grimaced. *That* wouldn't do. "The roof." The words had scarcely left her mouth before she winced. Why was she speaking of the roof, precisely now?

"Aye?" Nicholas cocked a brow.

She licked her lips, nervous, feeling quite unlike herself. "I will repay you, after the concert." Providing she wasn't a beggar on the streets by then. She glanced up into his face.

His gaze dropped to her mouth before meeting hers once again, and something in his eyes made her heart skip a beat.

"I assure you, that is quite unnecessary," he said.

Unnecessary? It took her a moment to remember the subject. Ah, the roof. "I do not accept charity, sir. I will be able to pay my debts, soon."

His sea-blue gaze returned to her lips.

It was dangerous to stand there, so close to him. A little on edge, she dipped her head. "Good day, my lord. I can find my way home from here."

She'd taken only three steps before he reached her side.

"If I didn't know better, I would think you are running from me." He chuckled.

"Hardly," she murmured as he once again captured her arm. "I merely wish to free you from an unnecessary obligation."

"Escorting you is neither unnecessary nor an obligation, lass," he replied in amusement. "Allow me to see you to your door."

She fell silent, keenly aware of his lithe, muscular form striding so easily at her side as they crossed the park. It was only when they stopped in the street before her music shop that she spoke again.

"There is the door," she said, tilting her head to the side, "scarce ten feet away."

Nicholas gave an easy laugh. "As politeness decrees, I should pay your father my respects ere I leave."

Olivia tensed and searched his face. "Surely, you have gathered my father isn't well, my lord."

There was only kindness in his eyes as he replied, "All the more reason to pay my respects." As she slipped her hand free of his arm, he reached for her fingers and gave them a squeeze before nodding at the roof. "At the very least, I must inspect the roofers' work."

She couldn't deny that request. "Very well."

He followed her through the shop and into the back. As she stepped into the parlor, Mrs. Lambert looked up, surprised.

"You're back, so soon?"

The soft tinkling of the piano spared Olivia a reply, but even without the distraction, she didn't need to answer. The tightening of Mrs. Lambert's mouth indicated that she understood that, again, something undesirable had happened.

"Soon, your luck will change, lass," the old woman muttered.

The tinkling of the piano stopped, and Olivia glanced over to her father. His fingers rested on the ivory keys.

"Olivia, child," her father said, "I swear, you've grown from this morning."

"Hardly, father." Olivia smiled and crossed the small room to straighten his hat before turning to Nicholas, who remained standing just inside the door. "Father, this is Lord Nicholas Blair."

Nicholas bowed and stepped into the room. "Good evening, Mr. Mackenzie."

Her father eyed him, puzzled. "Lord Blair…" Then, his eyes lit. "You came to the shop, did you not? Wanting music?"

Olivia blinked, surprised. Her father rarely remembered anyone. It had taken him a good year or more before he remembered Mrs. Lambert.

"Why, yes," Nicholas replied with a dry smile. "I purchased a variety of works." He shot Olivia an amused glance.

"Then, you play the violin?" her father queried.

"Nae."

"The piano?"

"Nae."

"What instrument, then?"

Olivia held her breath, tears misting her lashes at her father's clarity. That made twice of late and so close together.

"I must admit, Mr. Mackenzie, that I am not musically inclined," Nicholas responded with a rueful smile.

Her father knit his brows. "Why ever did you purchase the music, then?"

The way Nicholas' eyes locked onto hers made goosebumps rise on her arms, and looking straight into her eyes, he answered, "Mr. Mackenzie, your daughter has a way about her that's rather convincing."

Her father laughed, a deep laugh that Olivia hadn't heard in years. She turned to him, her throat closing with emotion, but as she watched, the mask of confusion fell once again.

"Olivia, child, you've grown," he murmured, then he began to play.

Olivia brushed tears away with the back of her hand. No matter. It was a gift to see him again, even for those few minutes.

"If you will excuse me," she heard Nicholas say. "I must inspect the roof."

"Why certainly, my lord," Mrs. Lambert replied. "I'll show you the way."

Olivia waited until their footsteps receded, then escaped to the front of the shop. A mountain of worries awaited her there, but strangely, she didn't want to think through them. She reached to the counter and, closing her eyes, rested her head on her arms, trying her best not to think, at all.

For a time, she merely listened to the tick-tock of the clock.

Nicholas's deep voice murmured by her side, "What worries you so?"

Slowly, Olivia lifted her head. "Opera singers." Indeed, they were at the root of her ills.

"Opera singers?"

"They're so blasted temperamental." She snorted a very unladylike snort.

He didn't appear to mind. He chuckled. "I have thought so myself, quite often."

Of course, a rake would respond so, but the nature of a rake's interest in an opera singer stood oceans apart from the nature of her own. Oddly, the thought irritated her more than it should have.

"Louisa is refusing to sing my concert, I hear." She forced her thoughts away from thoughts of rakes and back to her problems.

"Surely, there are other singers?" Nicholas lounged against the counter.

She glanced up at him. It was a mistake. The man held some wizardly power. Was it the way his broad shoulders and muscles strained his shirt? Or was it his tanned skin? His hands —he had such beautiful hands for a man.

"Olivia?"

Olivia. Not Miss Mackenzie. Her name on his lips made her shiver, even though he'd said her name before.

He caught her chin, his fingers searing like fire on her flesh.

"Do you ever accept help?" He tilted her face up toward his.

There was no mystery as to why Deborah had fallen. The man could melt an icicle with his eyes alone.

Feeling as if drugged with wine, she licked her dry lips and forced her gaze away. "They are my concerns, my lord. As for the roof—"

"Must you?" He closed the distance between them.

"Must I?" He smelled so delicious. She wanted him closer.

"Must you push me away?"

Her heart thudded at his words. She didn't want to. In fact, she wanted quite the opposite.

She wanted to kiss him, again.

CHAPTER 11

Raw attraction. Pure, raw attraction overwhelmed Nicholas as he found himself drowning in Olivia's expressive, jade-green eyes. She was beautiful, impossible to resist, like a fairy creature from another realm.

She stepped back, but an invisible string pulled him forward. He couldn't be part from her. No man could. Her lips called him like a siren. His hand lifted of its own will to run a thumb down the line of her jaw in a caress of the gentlest kind.

Her lashes dipped, the silent, slight movement a loud testament to the truth. She, like he, couldn't deny the raw attraction between them, ignited the moment their lips touched in his mother's garden.

She melted against him. For all her curves, she felt so fragile in his arms, yet he knew her to be a pillar of strength, a firebrand. Who moved first, he couldn't say. It didn't matter. Her lips touched his, soft, warm, satiny, and for a timeless, blissful moment, the world was right. The tip of her tongue teased his. The scent of her hair unleashed a deep desire to graze his teeth down the soft flesh of her neck.

Then, as quickly as it began, the magical moment ended.

"Forgive me," She abruptly pulled away.

Forgive me—not the exact words he wanted to hear. There would be no good ending to a sentence that began with 'forgive.'

"Why?" he asked, his voice hoarse even to his own ears.

She met his gaze fully, guilt suffusing her face. "Lord help me, how could I do this to my own cousin?"

Relief that her reluctance stemmed only from Deborah's lies warred with the dismay that she still believed them. Hadn't he managed to clear his name—even a bit? "I swear upon my soul that I never touched her."

Doubt clouded her eyes. At least part of her wanted to believe him, but that only meant the remainder didn't. He drew a sharp breath. Such was the price of his reputation. But then, he had only himself to blame.

Olivia swallowed and took another step back. "Still, this is a mistake."

By God, how he wanted to follow her, sweep her into his arms and kiss sense into those sweet lips. Instead, with every ounce of willpower, he forced himself to ask calmly, "How?"

Olivia rolled her eyes with a snort. "These stains, for a start." She held out her hands.

He caught her fingers and covered them with kisses.

She jerked her hand, but it was a half-hearted tug. "You are making this difficult."

"I am delighted to hear it," he chuckled, knowing the half-hearted tug spoke volumes.

"We stand an ocean apart," she breathed. "I am a working woman."

Nicholas dropped a slow kiss on her palm, his gaze locked with hers. Again, the tantalizing lashes dipped. Her breath hitched.

Then, she regained control and rolled her eyes. "I am serious."

"As am I," he murmured in his most seductive tone.

He was so close to kissing her, of tasting those lips again. Already, he could see her resolve waver.

Something leapt from the shelves above.

"What—" He jumped back.

Olivia laughed as a large tabby cat lifted its twitching tail and strolled down the counter.

"May I introduce you to Mr. Peppers?" She tickled the cat under his chin. "He's always sneaking in here, causing problems."

"Aye," he half growled in wholehearted agreement.

The cat flicked its ears in his direction, as if knowing what it had interrupted.

Olivia lifted the cat in her arms and strode to the door. "If you will excuse me, Lord Blair, I have a good day's work yet to do."

He watched her open the door and set Mr. Peppers on his four furry, interfering feet. She was putting distance between them. He sighed. The window of kissing her had shut—this time.

"As you wish, Miss Mackenzie."

NICHOLAS LOUNGED BACK IN HIS CHAIR AND EYED THE MAN seated across the table. Mr. Timms was the best in the snooping business, but he never failed to remind Nicholas of a Hertfordshire boar. Today, even more so. He looked damned uncomfortable in his waistcoat, a new one obviously worn for this occasion. The buttons strained with each word he spoke. Nicholas found himself watching the middle one, mentally wagering how long the thing had before it shot off across the hotel floor.

"I shall have an answer for you within the week, I am sure." Mr. Timms mopped his sweating brow for the fifth time.

"Discretion," Nicholas repeated, momentarily forgetting the button.

"Most assuredly, my lord," Mr. Timms wheezed. "Lady Deborah's reputation will not be harmed on my account." He hefted his bulk to the edge of his seat in preparation to leave.

"That's not all." Nicholas lifted a finger from the table to stop him.

The man sank back, the chair creaking with the shift of weight. The button held to the cloth, desperately. Nicholas gave the thing less than five minutes, and then focused his attention back on the man, his thoughts sobering. "In addition to the mystery of Lady Deborah's circumstances, I wish you to investigate those of another." He paused. Even though they were the only men in the hotel's parlor, he leaned closer and murmured, "Lord James Randall."

An eager gleam entered Mr. Timms' eye. "I have heard of the man. Much, to be truthful."

Nicholas cocked a curious brow. "I have a history with him."

"History?" Mr. Timms fished a pencil and parchment from his inner waistcoat pocket and waited.

"When I was a lad of twelve or so, he joined his father on the Randall estate, neighboring mine."

"Indeed." Mr. Timms jotted down a few words.

"For a few years, we were friendly, I suppose." Something about Randall had never set well with him, but in the remote location of their estates in Northern Scotland, Randall had been one of the few lads his age. "Of relevance are the events concerning...Henrietta."

"Henrietta?"

Henrietta Kendrick. Nicholas hadn't spoken of her in years, though he thought of her often enough. He closed his eyes and organized his thoughts. "I'd just finished school that year. I came home to a house party my mother was holding. Lady Kendrick and her daughter, Henrietta, were there. Along with Randall, of course. He'd been visiting daily. Henrietta was beautiful." More than beautiful. She was his first love. He'd fallen for her the moment he'd laid eyes upon her wealth of blonde curls.

"And?" Mr. Timms prompted when the silence lengthened.

"Ah, yes." Nicholas nodded, half in apology. "We both fell for Henrietta. Deeply. At first…" At first, she'd played them against each other. Then, she'd fallen hard. She'd chosen him. "We fell in love. We were to wed. We spoke of it often, though I hadn't proposed to her formally. The night of the card game. That's when Lord Randall made his move."

That night, he and Henrietta had exchanged harsh words. She'd wanted him to dance. He had wanted to play cards with Lord Witherspoon. He'd gone against her wishes and chosen the cards. When he finally left the card table in the wee hours of the morning, he discovered her gone. He thought she'd merely gone off to sleep.

The next morning, Lord Kendrick discovered Lord Randall in his daughter's bed. He ordered them wed within the week.

Nicholas closed his eyes.

He had been angry and refused to speak with her. He'd nearly left, but then, he met a woman. Anne or some such name. He bedded her as an act of vengeance. He then stayed at the blasted party, parading her in full view of Henrietta.

The day before the impromptu wedding, he had just finished his preparations to leave when a maid began screaming. He would never forget. How could he? He'd spent his every waking moment since, distracting himself with wine, women and song in an effort to banish the image of Henrietta's dangling feet, hanging from the barn rafters.

The wine and women had worked, for a time. Then, after

he'd made his peace with Henrietta, he kept to the habits of a rake. But now? Had he, at last, outgrown those distractions?

"Odd," Mr. Timms scribbled across the page as fast as he could.

Nicholas arched a brow. Just how much had he spoken aloud?

"Odd, Mr. Timms?"

"Strikes me odd how he went after Henrietta with such a vengeance that night," Mr. Timms answered. "Had to be more than pure jealousy, I'd say. Seemed in a wee bit of a rush to make his move on the night of the card game."

"Aye."

"What feelings did he show, when she died so unexpectedly?"

Nicholas thought back. Randall certainly hadn't appeared hurt. "Angry. Furious."

"Was she an heiress?" Mr. Timms glanced up. "Pardon my bluntness, my lord."

"Lord Kendrick was very well to do. At that time, anyway." He'd turned into quite the gambler after his daughter's untimely end. Who could blame the man?

"Right." Mr. Timms folded the parchment and tucked it into his waistcoat. "I will report the moment I have news, my lord."

"Very well." Nicholas rose and shook his hand.

After the man left, he returned to his chair. Mr. Timms had brought up an interesting point. He hadn't thought Lord Randall in need of money. The man lived in luxury, or, at least, appeared to do so. If he were poor, why the interest in Olivia? She clearly stood on the brink of poverty. Granted, she was the Duke of Lennox's granddaughter, but a disowned, disinherited one, and judging by the duke's behavior, that wasn't changing any time soon.

What business did Lord Randall have pursuing her? Unless...

Nicholas leaned back in his chair and closed his eyes. Unless, it was happening again. Were they both falling for the same woman? There was a difference, though. *This* lass was fierce and smart. She wasn't the kind to fall prey to Lord Randall's flattery…surely?

He expelled a breath and rose uneasily to his feet, recalling again the heartbreak on her face when she'd discovered herself robbed. If only she would let him help her. The roof obviously displeased her, but he held no regrets. At least, she was safe and dry, and as for her most pressing issue of the concert? Mr. Pitt, he'd taken care of. But the opera singer, Louisa?

His lip quirked as an idea formed. He was very well acquainted with one of the famous—if not the most famous—opera singers on the continent. One Florinda Marie de Bussonne, the Lark of Paris. Louisa Hamilton closer resembled the squawking of a chicken compared to Florinda's golden, dulcet notes.

If Olivia needed to fill the opera hall, at least, in that, he could oblige.

CHAPTER 12

Olivia placed the last envelope on the stack and rubbed her tired, reddened eyes. She'd written every opera singer she could think of, in England, Scotland, Ireland, on the continent and off. Even those associated with the smaller opera houses. And in each letter, she'd enclosed another, addressed to Louisa. Surely, one of the letters would find its way to the opera singer, and surely, once she'd read the heartfelt apology, along with the doubling of her fee, *surely, she would return?*

Olivia heaved a sigh. She'd started this venture for so many reasons, to honor her mother's memory and her father's—for what he had been—and to share the beauty of his music with the world. Everything had gone so splendidly…until she'd met Lord Randall.

If only she hadn't gone to Louisa's townhouse that night.

She leaned against the shop counter and tiredly lay her head down on her arms. She would rest…just for a minute.

The next thing Olivia knew, the rays of the morning sun warmed her cheek. Groggy, she lifted her head and glanced about. Her father was already playing the piano in the parlor, a sad, mournful melody. Olivia held still. Somehow, he knew.

She hadn't told him what day it was. How could she when he spent most of his days trapped in a dream?

Four years ago, to the very day, she'd been robbed of her parents. Four years ago, her mother had died. She straightened and grimaced. It was painful to visit her mother's grave, but even more painful to bear the burden alone. Still, she wasn't one to wallow in self-pity.

If she hurried, she could ready herself and visit her mother's grave before her appointment at the bank. The bluebells still bloomed along the river. They'd always been her mother's favorite. She would collect them along the way, as she always did, and lay them on her mother's gravestone. So many years, they'd collected them, together. She closed her eyes, almost hearing her mother's laughing, teasing voice. She hurried toward her room.

She'd just set foot on the bottom stair when she heard a knock on the shop door.

The piano stopped.

"Don't fret, Father," Olivia called. "I will get the door."

As the music resumed, Olivia hurried to the shop.

A glimpse through the curtains revealed a fine carriage parked on the street, as well as the fine blue silk of a woman's skirt as she waited by the door. The fine fall of lace from the sleeve revealed the gown to be an expensive one.

Quickly, Olivia lifted the latch. Deborah stood there with red, swollen eyes, clutching a letter to her breast.

Olivia's heart leapt into her throat. "What is it?"

Her cousin swallowed like a nervous bird, then swept inside. "It's all wrong, Olivia," she whispered. "You are not to blame. It's my doing."

"What is?" Olivia asked, alarmed as she followed her cousin to the counter.

"It's all wrong," Deborah choked. "I am at my wits' end."

She certainly looked it. There was a wild look of desperation about her that tore Olivia's heart. "If you tell me, I might be—"

"Grandfather cannot find out," Deborah interrupted. Then, dropped her hands to her waist. "Already, I have grown thicker, Olivia. Another month, there is no hiding."

She was right. Perhaps, there wasn't hiding, already.

The look in Deborah's eyes was a tortured one. "Oh, Olivia. It's the end. I will be disowned."

Olivia gave her cousin's hand a comforting squeeze. "I cannot see how grandfather can disown you, Deborah. He doesn't have another heir left now, does he?"

Deborah shook her head.

"Then, do not fret. We will think of something." Olivia drew a deep breath. "Nicholas will make this right."

"Nicholas," Deborah mouthed his name and then dropped the letter onto the counter. "Will you see he gets this? I do not know where he is staying. Do you?"

The sight of Nicholas's name on the envelope depressed her even more. Despite his claims to the contrary, something stood between him and Deborah. Why else would she write?

"Please, Olivia," Deborah begged, her voice scarcely above a whisper.

Olivia nodded, slowly.

The scrape of boots on the step outside interrupted further conversation, and as one, they turned as the door swung open.

Lord Randall entered.

He was persistent, to be sure, dressed as the perfect gentleman, suave and sophisticated as he strolled into the shop. He looped his silver-handled walking stick over his arm and doffed his hat.

"Lady Deborah. Miss Mackenzie. Good morning to you both."

It struck her then what irritated her about the man. He was perfect—too perfect. Orchestrated. Decidedly fake.

"I must go," Deborah blurted as she rushed to the door.

"Wait," Olivia called, but Deborah disappeared through the door.

Olivia grimaced. Her cousin was so high strung, but then, she had cause to be. It was entirely unfair she had to bear this burden alone. She pursed her lips, angry with Nicholas as well as herself for her own behavior with the man. It was only then that she noticed Lord Randall watching her every move.

"May I be of service?" he asked.

Again, such a gentlemanly, polished manner and speaking such kind words...so why did she want to smack the smile right off his face?

Forcing a polite smile, she murmured, "I believe I should ask that of you, my lord, as you have come into my shop."

He twirled his walking stick and sauntered to the counter. "I merely came by to offer the services of my carriage, Miss Mackenzie. Surely, you are attending Lady Kendrick's charity event?"

Even if she hadn't already planned to visit her mother's grave, she wouldn't have bothered to attend. What was the point? Doubtless, Elena's throat 'still hurt.'

"Thank you, Lord Randall, but I am fine," she replied. "I shan't be attending. I thank you for your kind offer." She owed him no further explanation.

Something about him hardened, almost imperceptibly—something chilling. So, he *did* have a temper, as gossip claimed.

Feeling a sudden need to put space between them, Olivia stepped behind the counter.

"I see," he murmured. "I thought you were attending." Again, the overly polished smile. "I thought merely to be of service, after hearing Lord Blair and your cousin conversing on the matter."

Olivia lifted a brow.

"But then, perhaps I misunderstood." He shrugged. "Such is

the way with those in love, they so often finish the sentences of the other. They could have been conversing about an entirely different matter."

The words hurt, even though they shouldn't, and as much as she didn't care for Lord Randall, in this, he had no cause to lie. So, Nicholas really *was* a rake. How could Lady Blair produce such a lying son?

Lord Randall smiled politely and leaned against the counter. "Now that I am here, I do believe I would care to purchase a song, after all. A gift for a pianist."

"Ah yes," Olivia replied through wooden lips. "Do you have a piece in mind?"

"Nae. Only, something popular. Special, perhaps. Something new?"

"I do believe I have something in the print room that might suffice," she said, seeking any excuse to escape his presence, if only for a moment. "If you would excuse me?"

"Most certainly, Miss Mackenzie." He nodded.

She slipped through the curtains. Refusing to let herself think of Nicholas, she hurried to the print room. The familiar scent of ink and paper soothed her rattled thoughts. After selecting several pages, she had calmed enough to return.

Lord Randall still stood by the counter where she'd left him.

"Perhaps one of these might suffice, my lord?" she queried with a distant smile.

He scarcely looked at them and selected the first. "This will do nicely."

"Then two shillings, my lord."

"Thank you, Miss Mackenzie." He dropped the coins onto the counter.

A sound behind her made Olivia turn. Her father stepped through the curtains.

"Olivia, child, my how you've grown." His hat slid off the back of his head.

The sight of his jagged scar was startling. Keenly aware of Lord Randall watching her every move, she quickly stepped up to her father and straightened his hat.

"Let's go, shall we, Father?"

"But, we have a customer, child," he objected.

"He's made his purchase, dear father." She pulled him toward the curtain.

Again, he stopped, but this time he looked her in the eye. "Your mother loves bluebells, child."

He knows what day it is.

"I know, Father," she whispered.

She saw the pain in his eyes, but only for a moment. Then, he was slipping between her fingers, retreating once again into his private world.

A movement from the corner of her eye reminded her that Lord Randall still waited. She tossed him a quick glance.

"If you will excuse me, my lord. I must see my father settled."

The man nodded, his face unreadable as he touched the brim of his hat. "Good day, Miss Mackenzie."

She watched him go, finding herself relieved when the door shut behind him. She turned back to her father and guided him to the parlor.

"Let's play some music, shall we?" she asked.

He said nothing as she led him back to his piano. Once again seated on his bench before the ivory keys, she watched as his world of music swallowed him.

For a time, Olivia stood by the door, resting her head against the frame. Her father was still there, despite what anyone else thought. She simply had but to listen to his music to know. Part of her couldn't blame him for giving up, for living in his world of notes. The other part of her, however, didn't agree. *She* was still here. She, his child, still needed him.

With a sigh, she brushed tears from her cheeks and headed

for her room. She changed into her best dress and glanced at her reflection in the mirror. She could only snort. She was so very far from the lady her mother had been. She inspected her ink-stained, calloused hands and shrugged as her father's music drifted up the stairwell.

She might not look like her mother, but she certainly had her determination and strength—enough strength for her father and herself, as well.

With a smile, Olivia picked up her bonnet, and by the time she returned to the shop, Mrs. Lambert had arrived.

"You will be off then?" the woman asked.

Olivia nodded. Mrs. Lambert knew her first stop and her second.

"Then good luck to you, lass."

Olivia sighed. With the banker, she would need it. Grimacing, she left and hurried to the river.

The day was warm, and the bluebells bloomed abundantly. In no time at all, she'd gathered a bouquet. Closing her eyes, she buried her face in the flowers, letting pleasant memories of the past parade through her mind as the soft petals brushed her cheek. Almost, she could hear her mother's sweet laughter once again, playing a soprano to her father's bass as he sang while working the press.

Then, as swiftly as the memories came, they faded.

Silently, she made her way to the kirk, a time-worn building of stone surrounded by a black-iron fence. She slipped through the gate and picked her way past the older, ivy-covered gravestones, their stone faces weathered and covered with lichen. As she stepped around an old mausoleum, Olivia drew up short.

A man knelt at her mother's grave. Startled, she stepped back, taking cover behind the mausoleum's cold stones and then slowly, peered around the corner. The man's shoulders shook as he covered his face with his hands. Then, he shifted his weight, revealing gray hair under his hat. As she watched, his head turned to the side.

Her heart stopped. Surely, her eyes deceived her. How could her grandfather, the Duke of Lennox, be kneeling at her mother's grave...weeping? He rose stiffly to his feet and brushed the tears from his cheeks, brusquely, as if they had no right to be there. She could only watch in open astonishment.

Then, he turned on his heel and she drew fully back behind the mausoleum. Her grandfather was difficult as it was. She harbored not a single doubt that he would be beyond displeased to discover she'd witnessed his private moment.

As the duke approached, she inched around the tomb, keeping out of his line of sight. He didn't even glance her way. He strode out of the cemetery with a purposeful step and disappeared around the corner of the kirk. For a moment, she was tempted to dash after him. Why had he come? Why now? Why acknowledge her mother *now*? After so many years?

Anger warred with confusion. Then, the ephemeral scent of bluebells reminded her of her true purpose for being here. She wouldn't dishonor her mother's memory. Shoving all thoughts of her grandfather aside, she turned her feet to her mother's grave.

"As I have said a dozen times before, it is unseemly for a man of my position to discuss business matters with a...a...a..."

Olivia sat across from the banker, but she no longer listened. Husband. Again. The banker never failed to remind her that he wished only to do business with her husband. He had only dealt with her so far out of courtesy and respect to her father, but such courtesy could only last so long.

"Do we have an understanding?" the man asked.

Olivia stood. "Thank you for your time, Mr. Trent."

There was no use in prolonging the displeasure for either of them. Without a word more, she swept out of the bank and marched across the street.

For the first time, she felt the sharp pang of visceral fear. What if she *couldn't* make Mr. Pitt's last payment? She would have to sell every sheet of music she had, and at a discount, to come up with the money needed…but what if it wasn't enough? And what if Louisa didn't return? What if her dream of revealing her father's music to the world remained only that…a dream?

A man stepped into her path.

"Pardon me, sir," she muttered, sidestepping him.

A hand dropped onto her arm. "Olivia?"

She looked up, startled.

It was Nicholas.

CHAPTER 13

NICHOLAS YAWNED FROM THE COMFORT OF HIS CARRIAGE AS THE bank came into view. It was an impressive building, granite, with six Corinthian columns topped with statues. Exactly what they were of, he hadn't a clue. No doubt, they represented money in some shape or fashion—massive good luck charms for the wealthy bankers lurking within.

As the carriage rolled forward, a familiar shade of auburn hair stormed down the bank steps and crossed the street. He'd recognize her anywhere. Olivia. He rapped the window but leapt from the carriage before the coachman pulled rein. He caught up with her as she turned toward Glasgow Green.

"Pardon me, sir," she muttered as he stepped into her path.

"Olivia?"

She blinked and looked up. For the briefest of moments, her eyes widened with what could only be pleasure. Then, a mask fell over her face and her bonny green eyes shuttered.

"My lord," she murmured.

The tone was so formal, he winced.

"Might I offer you a ride?" He hooked his thumb over his shoulder at the carriage now waiting across the street.

"No, thank you," she replied at once. "I shan't keep you from Deborah."

He lifted a puzzled brow. Deborah? Again? "I confess, that is not a name I expected to hear—especially after our last meeting."

Olivia lifted her chin, giving her head a little toss, and for a moment, he lost all track of what she was saying. He wanted to kiss her again.

"There is no need to hide the fact you're truly lovers," she snapped.

"What the devil?" Aye, perhaps it was high time he simply *showed* her the truth, kiss some sense into those plump, pink lips.

She closed her eyes and puffed a breath, blowing the hair from her face. "Forgive me. I am out of sorts. Dealing with the bank darkens my mood."

"Understandable, I assure you," he granted, then drew his brows into a line. "But this nonsense of Deborah must end."

"Truly, I only wish you the best," she replied. "Since we are to be relatives—"

He caught her shoulder. "I thought you were of the under-standing that Deborah spoke of me falsely. Surely you could see that when we spoke with her?"

"Lord Randall informed me that he sees the both of you together, often enough—"

He couldn't bear to hear more. "What tripe is this?" He snorted with contempt. "Lord Randall? Good Lord, the man is at it again." Mr. Timms couldn't investigate fast enough.

Olivia hesitated. "At what, again?"

He clenched his jaw. "The man is a liar, lass. Come. Shall we discuss this in the privacy of my carriage?"

She rooted herself to the ground. "I have much to do—"

"Please, Olivia. All is not as it seems, I assure you."

When she heaved a breath, he knew he'd won and, minutes

later, they were safely settled in his carriage, with the coachman given orders to take the longest route back to her printing shop.

As the carriage rolled forward, Nicholas began, "Years ago, both Randall and I fell for the charms of the same lass, one Henrietta Kendrick."

"Lady Kendrick's daughter?" Her lashes fluttered in recognition.

So, she knew something of the matter. "You have heard of her?"

"Lady Kendrick spoke often how her daughter died of a fever days before her wedding. Such a tragedy."

A fever? Of course. Polite society could hardly tolerate the truth of the lass hanging herself from the rafters in a barn.

He repeated the same story he'd told Mr. Timms. She listened with rapt attention, never interrupting. When he'd finished, she remained quiet.

Finally, he broke the silence with, "I beg you, Olivia. Do not trust Lord Randall. He is hiding something."

She responded with a muffled snort. "Have no fear. The man disturbs me."

Aye, she was so different than Henrietta. She was a fighter, a lioness.

Then, she looked him straight in the eye. "As for Deborah, you must make things right."

He shot her a withering look. "As for Deborah, I am truly helping the lass, I assure you, but I will not wed her when I am *not* the father. A week, Olivia. A week and I should know more." Mr. Timms would, no doubt, uncover the truth, and once uncovered, the next step would become clearer.

"A week, then," she agreed.

Further conversation ended with their arrival at the music shop. He helped her down, again savoring the light touch of her fingers on his hand, and as ever, his eyes fell to the sway of her hips and the wide ribbon spanning her waist as she took her leave.

"The hotel, my lord?" his coachman asked when he turned back to his carriage.

He nodded and returned to his seat. It was fitting that Olivia was in the music business. Her body was the finest instrument and, soon, would be his for the playing. He lifted his lip in a private smile. Soon, she'd wear a ribbon and nothing else. He felt himself grow hard at the thought.

The thought of visiting Demelza flashed across his mind, the thought quickly followed by revulsion. He knew what the reaction meant. He was falling for Olivia. Hard. He focused his gaze out the window. In the not-so-distant past, the thought of falling for a woman would have made him run. This time, he wanted a different ending…a permanent one. He slouched back into his seat, letting his thoughts wander over Olivia's roof, her endeavors with the concert, and, of course, her splendid curves.

In less time than he'd thought possible, the carriage arrived at his hotel, and he'd no sooner stepped inside than Mr. Timms' bulky form rose from one of the leather chairs beside the window.

"My lord." The man bowed.

The movement threatened to pop his straining waistcoat buttons. With amusement, Nicholas noticed the top button already missing.

"I have news," the man announced.

"So soon?" *Good.* "Please, join me in my rooms."

Neither man spoke until they settled safely behind the closed door of Nicholas's private sitting room.

"Lord Randall," Mr. Timms began at once, "seems to have an interesting financial situation."

"Interesting? How?"

"His estate is in ruins, owed entirely to the bank, yet he has founded many charities, my lord."

Charities? Not bloody likely. Randall was the least charitable person to walk the streets of Glasgow. "Ridiculous."

"I am inclined to agree with you, my lord, but I am still inspecting the matter." Mr. Timms folded his pudgy hands across the vast expanse of his belly. "As for Lady Deborah…"

Nicholas tapped his finger in anticipation.

"Hers is a common enough plight. Until five months ago, she was keeping close company to Lord Piers Deveraux, second son to the Comte de Gercourt. A man I believe you know well?"

"Piers?" Nicholas drew a sharp breath in surprise. "He never mentioned her. Of course, I haven't seen him since Paris—last fall, I believe."

Mr. Timms nodded. "Their affair was of a whirlwind nature, and from all appearances, a genuine one, despite Lord Deveraux's passing distraction to the Lady Marie Rochambeau."

"Passing distraction?"

"Lady Deborah discovered them, ahem…shall we say…in a compromised position?" Mr. Timms mopped his face.

"Caught them in bed, eh?" Nicholas queried dryly.

"Aye, my lord." The investigator nodded. "Her heart broke. She left Paris and returned home to her grandfather's estate, outside Glasgow. There, shall we say, she succored her heart with the attentions of the stable lad."

"The stable lad?" Nicholas repeated, surprised. So, the stable lad had fathered the child? Deborah's desperation could now be understood. Then, he recalled Mr. Timms' first comment. "You said their affair—Piers' affair with Deborah—appeared genuine in nature?"

"The man is distraught. He pines for her in Edinburgh, according to those with knowledge of the matter."

Nicholas strode to the window and crossed his arms. Pined for her, did he? Genuine? Genuine enough to forgive her for making the same mistake Piers had himself? He drummed his fingers on his arms.

Well, there was only one way to find out. He'd have to speak with the man himself.

CHAPTER 14

"DAMNATION!" OLIVIA SWORE AND SUCKED HER FINGERTIP. "NOT again."

She kicked the foot of the printing press bolted to the floor. Pain shot through her toe. Fine. That wasn't the best of decisions, but she'd just smashed her finger for the third time that day and she hadn't slept a wink last night. She'd stayed up to print her entire paper supply in a desperate bid to raise the needed money.

At the first of the week, she'd lowered the price of every sheet of music she possessed, and thanks to Mrs. Reid, the silk merchant's wife and the loudest gossip on the street, word spread. A new class of customers began trickling into her shop, primarily composed of the daughters of Glasgow's merchants.

Still, she'd sold more music than she thought possible. She had even made a small profit. Small, not enough to pay the wages of a shop lad, but since she was doing the work herself, it was enough to fuel her with a cautious optimism. Perhaps, just perhaps, she might make enough to cover the last payment, after all.

As for news of Louisa? She scowled. She'd received only

two responses, both claiming no knowledge of the opera singer's whereabouts, but promises to deliver the letter should that change.

The press groaned, and she jerked back her hand, narrowly avoiding the frame as it fell into place. At last, she was ready to print. She picked up the paper. There was so much to do. A little later in the morning, she had a few deliveries to make, one to Colonel Buids' wife, only four townhouses away from her grandfather's.

The thought of her grandfather summoned an image of him kneeling at her mother's grave. She released the Devil's Tail and rubbed the back of her neck. She couldn't banish the image of the man from her mind. Again and again, at the oddest times, she saw his shaking shoulders, the angle of his head, rife with grief.

She thinned her lips. Well, it was too late for sorrow *now*. He should have made peace with his daughter while she lived instead of waiting to whisper words on her gravestone.

As much as she wanted to check after Deborah's welfare—she hadn't heard from her in nearly a week—she wasn't ready to risk seeing her grandfather again. Not yet.

As for Nicholas, the man had vanished from her shop, but then, such was the nature of a rake. That fact bothered her much more than it should.

"How could such a sweet, sweet lady give birth to such a man?" she asked acidly, for what must have been the twentieth time, half hoping that voicing the condemnation would somehow chase the man from her mind.

Of course, it didn't work. It only seemed to summon visions of his blue eyes. She closed her eyes and rested her head against the cap of the press. What kind of wanton woman was she to lust after her cousin's soon-to-be husband?

With a growl, she forced herself to return to her task, and an hour later, she stood over the counters in the print room, eyeing the drying sheets with satisfaction, but only for a minute. She had deliveries to attend.

She'd just finished tying the last bundle in the front of the shop when Mrs. Lambert breezed in through the curtains.

"My dear *child*." The woman's mouth formed an 'o' of surprise upon taking in Olivia's appearance. "Have you been up all night?"

Olivia answered with a grin and a yawn.

Mrs. Lambert thinned her lips, her mole hairs seeming to disapprove, as well.

"I wil sleep tonight," Olivia promised as she pushed past the woman and headed upstairs.

After she'd changed quickly, splashed water on her face, and dragged a comb through her hair, she ran back down the stairs and collected the music.

Four deliveries. She'd save the last for Colonel Buids' wife. She'd scarcely gone a dozen yards from her door when she heard her name. She prevented herself from turning, just in time.

Lord Randall.

She quickened her pace and ducked into a narrow alley where his carriage couldn't follow. Not only did Nicholas's warnings of the man ring true, she knew in her heart that he was up to no good. Not wanting to waste a thought on the man, she breathed deeply of the fresh, early summer air and hurried through Glasgow's streets.

In short order, she delivered all four bundles, with the colonel's being the last. As she stepped into the street to turn homewards, she paused. She was so close to her grandfather's townhouse. It wouldn't hurt to pay a quick visit to Deborah… and if she found Nicholas there? She expelled a huff.

"Well, if that's where he's been hiding, then, all is as it should be," she muttered, even as her heart disagreed.

Twenty minutes later—twenty minutes of indecision—she

finally stood outside her grandfather's townhouse, looking for signs of Nicholas's carriage and finding none.

Relief washed over her as she lifted the door's brass knocker.

On the third knock, the door opened. "Lady Deborah is not at home," the maid bobbed in answer to her inquiry.

Olivia pursed her lips. "Will she return soon?"

"If you will kindly come inside, I shall inquire, Miss." The maid held the door open wide.

She led Olivia down the hall and to the sitting room, and after seeing her inside, quickly left. Olivia stepped gingerly inside. It was a beautiful room. Of course, she would expect nothing less from the Duke of Lennox. She glanced about. From the gleaming gold brocade couches to the overstuffed chairs, the room seemed too new, too perfect, as if never used. Even the heavy silk drapes and crystal beaded chandelier suspended in the center of the ceiling appeared as only beautiful facades, hardly a home. Nothing like the comfort of her tawdry, rundown parlor.

She grinned at the comparison. Hardly in a mood to sit, she wandered to the small collection of portraits hanging over a side table that displayed a magnificent Chinese vase. One portrait caught her eye, a small one. Peering closer, she realized with a start that it was a depiction of her mother.

"Why are you here?" a gruff bass grated.

Olivia whirled as the Duke of Lennox strode into the room, his brows drawn into a thick line of displeasure. One would never have guessed him a man to weep over his disowned daughter's grave.

"Are you struck dumb?" he asked waspishly.

Olivia snorted. "Forgive me. I merely sought to reconcile the man I saw in the graveyard with the man before me now," she answered, the truth lending her voice a deeper strength.

He froze, then slowly resumed his walk to the window. He

reached it and turned. "It is high time you and I came to an understanding."

"Pardon?"

He didn't care for the challenge in her tone. That much was obvious by the dark roil in his eyes. "I will not have you embarrassing the family name."

Family name? The ship named 'Family' had sailed years ago. "Pardon?" she repeated, this time with more than a touch of contempt.

"You must marry," he said in clipped tones.

So, another pompous man sought to order her about? "I must inform you that I am not inclined to do so—not that my marriage is any concern of yours."

He clamped his jaw. "It is quite unseemly—quite—that a lady of your position seeks to run a venture such as printing music. Clearly, that is the domain of men."

Olivia laughed outright.

Her grandfather's head snapped back.

"Let me lay your concerns to rest, then," she chuckled dryly. "First, I can run a press better than most, I assure you, be they man or woman. Second, I am no concern of yours. The word 'family' does not exist between us. Therefore, I am hardly a lady."

"Indeed, you are not," he replied in cold disdain.

His words didn't even hurt. Olivia shrugged. "Your words have no power over me," she replied with a pert smile.

He blinked.

"Are you expecting me to faint? Wither? Wilt?" she challenged.

The duke's brows furrowed. "My reputation—

"Of which I care not a whit," Olivia inserted.

"Randall is acceptable," he finished abruptly.

The change of subject took her by surprise. "Pardon?"

"I will provide the dowry—"

"Pardon?"

"Do *not* interrupt me," his voice thundered in the room.

Her anger erupted. "And, *you*, do *not* think to control my life," she raised her voice in turn. "I will marry if and when I please, and very most certainly, *not* at your command."

He drew back as if she'd slapped his cheek, apparently unused to challenges.

She didn't care. Caught in a depth of anger she'd never before experienced, she planted her hands on her hips. "Lord help me, but do I understand you correctly? Dare you, and Lord Randall—of all men to walk the Earth—dare speak of *my* marriage? The impudence, the pure audacity..." her voice trailed away, speechless.

"These are men's concerns," the duke spat.

"Oh? My own life isn't my concern?" The fury boiling in Olivia grew hotter by the second. How dare her grandfather speak to Lord Randall...and how dare Lord Randall speak with her grandfather? Suddenly, the man's constant snooping around her shop became clear.

"Never," she vowed. "I will never wed the man. *Ever.*"

"His title could restore some semblance of respectability to a woman of your position," came her grandfather's curt reply.

Olivia rolled her eyes. "I have no interest in joining the ranks of those coldhearted, uncaring..." she faltered as an unwanted image of his shaking shoulders in the graveyard slipped through her thoughts.

She fell silent, her anger drained.

The duke didn't move.

For a time, only the creaking of the carriages on the street outside came between them. At last, the duke stalked to a walnut cabinet in the corner of the room, took a key from his pocket, and twisted it into the uppermost locked drawer. He opened the doors and pulled out a small, carved box.

"This means nothing to you?" He held the box up as he turned to face her.

Olivia shook her head. Slowly, he joined her. When he reached her side, he extended his hand and opened the lid of the box.

"This was your mother's heritage before she let pride get in her way," he rasped.

A small ceramic shoe glistened on a bed of white velvet. Sapphires and diamonds encrusted the heel and the upper edges. Where one might expect a bow or a buckle near the toe, a sapphire, as large as a Robin's egg, rested instead, surrounded by a ring of diamonds catching the stray rays of light filtering into the room.

Olivia knew what it was. The Blue Slipper.

"Your mother's pride kept you poor, Olivia. Her pride prevented you from a proper education, one that befits a lady. Your mother's pride—her obstinance—condemned you to the lower echelons of society." He spoke slowly, ominously.

For a suspended moment in time, Olivia simply stared at the small shoe, lying on its velvet bed.

The lid abruptly snapped shut and her grandfather spun on his heel to return the box to the cabinet. As he twisted the key in the lock, he said, "Walk away from this madness of *An Enchanted Summer Evening*. Sponsoring a concert is no place for a woman. *Sell* your shop, if you must. Wed Randall and gain a title. Then, you can return to your proper place in society." He faced her, his craggy face an unreadable mask. "It is simple, Olivia. It's time you walked away from your father and his dreams."

Walk away from her father? Olivia's chin lifted. "Never. You dare judge my mother? Pride, you say? Obstinance? You are so wrong, so very, very wrong. My mother's *love* taught me the meaning of a true family and a home." She eyed the soulless perfection of the room around her as well as the man, then added, "Clearly, that is something you will never understand. True love cannot be bought." She whirled and headed for the door.

She was three feet away from it when her grandfather's hand dropped on her shoulder. "Accept Randall," he urged. "Then, I can bestow upon you a dowry."

Olivia didn't bother turning around. "At the price of my father? Never. Yet even more so, from myself. I detest Lord Randall. I will never wed the man."

"I will not give you a penny otherwise."

This time, she did turn. With a laugh combined with a humph of disdain, she retorted, "Never have I asked from you a single penny. I will most certainly not start now. I will make my own way—without your help. That, I promise you."

She stormed out of the sitting room, down the hall and out the front door. It wasn't until she reached the edge of Glasgow Green that she realized she'd left without garnering news of Deborah's time of return. She expelled a breath. Oh, well, it couldn't be helped. She would find a different way to reach her cousin, one that avoided any meeting with the cantankerous, judgmental Duke of a grandfather.

Just what the man was up to fair puzzled her. Why care now? Why throw a husband and a dowry in her path? Did her concert hurt his reputation that badly? She smiled, coldly. If it did, then she'd double her efforts. She'd do everything possible to make *An Enchanted Summer Evening* happen. She'd even bally well sell the press if she had to.

The moment she set foot in the park, another hand dropped on her arm. She jerked free and glanced up, surprised and affronted and very much irritated at men manhandling her arm and shoulder as they pleased. To her great annoyance, Lord Randall peered down at her with a pleased, smug expression.

Pleased, was he? Unable to stop the anger from erupting,

she snapped without preamble, "You have spoken of me to the duke?"

His brows twitched, obviously not expecting such a direct response. "Forgive me, am I out of order?" he asked after a moment.

"If you're asking if you are out of order discussing my future with the duke—without my consent, mind you—then the answer is yes." She looked him straight in the eye. "The duke does not speak for me. You have been misinformed."

Olivia didn't miss the tic of his jaw muscle nor the fleeting flare of his nostrils. The rumors of his temper were obviously true. Her anger deepened all the more. How *dare* her grandfather seek to forge a union with a foul-tempered man with a title—simply for the sake of *his own reputation.* Small wonder Deborah was distraught about confessing her situation to him.

"Olivia, please." Lord Randall stepped closer.

So now, it was 'Olivia,' was it? Did he really think she'd swoon over him, fall for him that easily? She wasn't Louisa's kind.

"If you will excuse me, Lord Randall," she murmured in frosty tones. "I must be going."

As she turned, he reached out as if to touch her again.

She stopped him with a withering glare. "Good *day,* my lord."

She marched down the garden path, ignoring his calling of her name. Really, the man was a mystery. What did he expect of her? That she'd turn around and run into his arms?

She arrived at the shop, out of sorts, and slammed the front door shut.

The bang brought Mrs. Lambert through the curtains. "Oh, it's you, lass." She wiped her hands on her apron. "I sold a song while you were out. Put the coins in the box there." Her mole hairs pointed the way.

"Thank you, Mrs. Lambert." Olivia grimaced. One sheet. Still, one sale was better than none.

She opened the box and emptied the coins into her palm. Eight shillings in all. Her gaze caught on one of the coins. It was bent. She squinted closer. It was the coin Lord Randall had given her. Odd. Bent, like the coin stolen from her box under the floorboard.

Strange.

What were the odds she'd possess two bent shillings?

With a sigh, she shrugged the thought away and headed to the print room to work. She had to bolster her sales. It was time to advertise in the paper, but first, she had to bind the music she'd printed.

MORNING ARRIVED DREARY AND UNSEASONABLY COLD, BUT FOR all the gloom, the shop bustled with customers. Olivia smiled, pleased. Her last newspaper announcement had proved fruitful. She eyed her box beneath the counter. While it wasn't overflowing, she was pleased with the week's sales.

A gasp circled a group of young women perusing the music near the window.

"Who is it?"

"A noble—"

"Look at the *carriage*."

"The horses—so white."

A pang of disappointment stabbed Olivia. White horses ruled out Nicholas. Rolling her eyes at herself, she craned her neck toward the window. She couldn't see much beyond the glossy back of a coach with a gilded hub and gold-painted wheels.

"He's so braw, handsome," someone whispered.

Olivia furrowed her brows. The 'handsome' ruled out her

grandfather, and she'd like to say, Lord Randall, as well—but they were obviously judging on looks alone, not personality. Doubtless, Lord Randall had arrived to foist himself upon her, *again*.

She strode to the door and yanked it open just as a footman —a decidedly dashing and handsome one, resplendent in the Duke of Lennox's livery—stretched his hand toward the knob.

The man blinked, then bowed. "His Grace, the Duke of Lennox, requests your presence, at once, for the afternoon and dinner."

A chorus of oohs and ahhhs circled behind Olivia as she stared at the footman, surprised. What game was her grandfather playing now?

"Not bloody likely," she retorted.

Gasps replaced the soft coos behind her. She didn't care. She wouldn't dance to her grandfather's tune. She tossed her head, but then, an image of his shoulders shaking as he knelt by her mother's grave slipped through her thoughts. Damn him. Why did family have to be so complicated?

A twinge of guilt made her wince. "I beg your pardon." She eyed the footman ruefully. The poor man wasn't at fault. "My grandfather brings out my worst manners."

A gleam of amusement entered the man's eye. He obviously commiserated. He bowed again, this time, a full bow of respect. "Forgiven, my lady. Think no more of it."

Lady? Olivia arched a dry brow. "However, I must still decline. I have work."

"You aren't going?" someone blurted in a loud whisper.

Olivia rolled her eyes. "Good day." She nodded at the man. He hesitated.

Oliva arched a brow. "And?"

"His Grace…is not used to being denied." The man eyed her in what could only be awe.

"Indeed?" Olivia chuckled, then dusted her hands on her

shop apron. "Well, most likely, this will be a good experience for him, then. Good day, sir."

The man nodded, turned smartly on his heel, and strode toward the carriage as Olivia closed the door.

"Dinner with the Duke of Lennox?" the women hissed behind their fans.

Olivia suppressed a snort. She would eat carrots and hay with the horses first. Of course, she felt sorry for Deborah, but—

She paused and frowned, seeing her cousin in her mind's eye, standing by the counter. She'd been so distraught. Olivia drew her brows into a deeper frown as a thought hovered on the edge of her recollection. Deborah had visited her—

Good Lord. Deborah had asked her to deliver a letter to Nicholas.

Olivia choked, horrified. She'd clean forgotten. She dashed around the counter, searching the floor and the shelves beneath. Where had the damn thing gone?

"Mrs. Lambert? Mrs. Lambert?" She darted behind the curtains and raced to the parlor.

The woman looked up from her darning. "What's happened?"

"A letter…last week…" Olivia swallowed. "A letter on the shop's counter. Have you seen it?"

"Last week?" Mrs. Lambert rolled her eyes. "Lordy, child. I scarce remember yesterday. I am not going to remember a week or more." She shook her head. "Who was to receive it?"

"Nicholas—Lord Blair."

"Ah, I see." A gleam entered her aged eyes, then she shook her head. "Nae. Can't say I have seen it, lass."

Olivia expelled a long breath and winced. Deborah had trusted her. She closed her eyes. Well, there was nothing she could do but confess the truth to her cousin. The buzz of the shop faded as she headed back to the print room for a sheet of paper and a quill.

She'd compose a quick letter to Deborah, asking to meet.
Bad news was best told face-to-face.

COME TO THE LOUNGE AT THE CIRCULATING LIBRARY ON ST.
Vincent's Street. Noon. Wednesday.

The words had kept Olivia on pins and needles for two
days. For two days, she'd replayed in her mind just how she'd
confess her carelessness.

She eyed herself in the mirror with a wry grimace. There,
by the knee…a splatter of ink. No matter how hard she tried,
ink found its way to her skirts. There were times she almost
believed the tales that swirled around the print shops, of the
Devil's minions switching the type in the middle of the night
and other such mischiefs. Her shop was different, though.
Instead of changing the type, her shop minions scampered up
the stairs each night to dance on her clothes. She cocked a
brow. Indeed, this stain *did* resemble a tiny foot print.

"Well, there's naught to be done," she grumbled.

The other dresses stood in worse repair, but then, with the
weight of her confession, an ink-stained dress was the least of
her concerns. She hurried down the stairs but paused in the
parlor door long enough to exchange farewells with Mrs.
Lambert before she tied the ribbons of her hat and hurried out
the back door. Deborah would be upset, of course. She'd
entrusted Olivia to deliver her letter, and judging by her
behavior that day, a letter of some import. Wincing, Olivia
hurried down the narrow, walled alley that ran between her
row of townhouses and the row behind.

A letter to Nicholas, no less.

She clenched her fingers. Really, it was no surprise Deborah
had fallen for the man. In his company, it was so easy to fall for

him…but, such was the power of a rake. They were impossible to resist and even harder to push from the mind.

Olivia bit her lip. She'd tried so very hard not to think of him, but it was fair difficult. She should never have kissed him, yet truly, given half a chance, she knew she was tempted to kiss him again—despite the fact he was, most likely, her cousin's lover.

She rolled her eyes and hurried down the alley. She should be ashamed. What kind of girl was she? She had more pressing concerns, from concert halls to wayward opera singers. She hurried past Mrs. Prescott's garden with its apple tree growing over the wall, nearly blocking the alley's exit.

As she stepped around the low-hanging branch, a man's voice called from behind, "Olivia."

She turned. She barely had time to register the caller as Nicholas before he caught her about the waist. Lord help her. His head was dipping. She shouldn't kiss him, but how could she not? From the way he splayed his fingers on the base of her spine to the teasing way he caught her lip, it was so clear he knew her body better than she did.

CHAPTER 15

Nicholas whirled Olivia behind the apple tree's overhanging branches and walked her back against the alley's brick wall. She felt so right in his arms. She looked so right, as well, with her large green eyes wide with surprise and the leaves from the branches crowning her hair. Her lips parted, drawing his attention to their plump softness and then, he couldn't stop himself.

He dropped his head, his lips catching hers.

He hadn't planned on kissing her. After all, she'd yet to believe him anything other than a rake. A kiss—especially the kind he was giving her—would only underscore that belief, but how could a man eschew such temptation? It was nigh impossible. He slid his palm down her spine and splayed his fingers low, drawing her close against him. By George, she belonged with him. He was a man ensnared.

He teased her lips apart and then, for a sweet moment, his tongue found heaven, dancing with hers.

Then, her palms came up against his chest.

"Nae," she gasped, pushing him back. Her eyes locked on

his. "Nae. I must stop this. I am ashamed. There, stay at arm's length."

Arm's length? Nicholas suppressed a sigh. Of course. Deborah still stood between them. Soon, she wouldn't be...and then? Then, he'd kiss those lips to his heart's content—and more.

"Where have you been?" Olivia's tart demand sifted through his thoughts.

Nicholas arched an amused brow. The wee firebrand was taking him to task, as if he were a child. His gaze swept her curves as she stood before him, fists planted firmly on his hips and her chin held high.

"I've been to Edinburgh." He couldn't say more. Not yet. Not until he'd assured himself that Deborah cared for Lord Deveraux as much as the man still truly loved *her*.

"Edinburgh?" Olivia frowned.

Nicholas slowly leaned forward until they stood eye to eye. "Soon, I shall absolve myself in your eyes, Olivia. Then, there will be no reason for you to resist."

"Resist?" she repeated, then blushed.

Aye, she knew that resistance was only a word between them. If he kissed her again, she'd respond, and right willingly. He could see it in her eyes.

He drew a long breath. How he longed to sweep her into his arms and carry her to his bed. His cock stirred. With a wry twist of his lip, he stepped back. Aye, there would be time enough to taste the delights of her flesh. Soon. Oddly, with Olivia, he wanted the experience to be perfect.

"Well, then." Olivia tossed her head, her ringlets bouncing.

Nicholas chuckled. Soon. Soon, he'd taste that fire in bed. "And where are you off to, Miss Mackenzie?"

"I am off to the circulating library," she replied with a prim purse of her lips.

"I shall be delighted to accompany you," he responded,

offering his arm. "But the circulating library? I hadn't thought you one to idle the day with such frivolities."

Her mouth tightened, and he felt her grow tense under his arm. "I am meeting Deborah there, in the lounge."

Ah, Deborah. "Then it is fortunate we meet. I must speak with Deborah on a matter most urgent." The woman's happiness depended upon it.

"I see," Olivia murmured, turning all at once distant.

Nicholas curled his lip. "It isn't at all what you think. I've told you from the start, I never touched the lass, but I do believe I hold the recipe for her happiness in my keeping. I hope, for Deborah, to offer her a happy end to this tragedy."

"Truly?" Olivia lifted her brows.

"Aye, and then, you and I shall talk." Not that after the first few words there would be much talking involved—especially if he got his hands on a ribbon.

"My lord?"

She was looking at him rather suspiciously. Nicholas grinned. If she only knew half of what he'd been thinking of late, she'd blush to her very toes. As his cock began to harden, he forced his thoughts to safer territory.

"How has the music business been, of late?"

"Well enough, I suppose," Olivia obliged as they crossed the street. "Soon, I shall pay Mr. Pitt his fee."

"And your opera singer?"

Olivia thinned her lips. "I am sure I will hear from her soon."

So, the woman still played games, did she? Olivia's concert deserved far better than the likes of Louisa. He'd never cared for the woman, though she'd tried to entice him more than once. Thoughts of Louisa reminded him that he'd yet to hear from Florinda. Perhaps, he should send Mr. Timms to Paris.

A pleasant silence fell and Nicholas found himself drawn into the present. Truly, what more could a man desire than the warm sun on the back of his neck and a woman, such as Olivia, on his arm?

All too soon, the white stone-faced building housing the circulating library loomed before them. Nicholas paused and waited for a lumbering coach to creak past before escorting Olivia up the half dozen steps to the brass-handled doors.

"Shall I leave you—" he began.

"Lord Blair!" a soft voice whooshed in surprise at his elbow.

Nicholas glanced down to see Deborah only a few paces behind.

"My lady." Nicholas politely touched the brim of his hat.

Deborah searched his face, as if expecting more. Then, her eyes darted to Olivia.

"Deborah." Olivia sucked in a breath. "Let's speak in the lounge, shall we?"

"Certainly, to be sure."

"Then, shall I leave the two of you now?" Nicholas smiled, reaching for the brass handles.

Deborah choked. "Heavens no, you *must* come, Lord Blair," she whispered, again searching his face. "I've a private lounge, ready and waiting. It's…time, isn't it?"

Time? Nicholas bowed and opened the door, allowing them to pass before him.

Books surrounded him on every side, along with a plethora of young ladies, most giggling and gossiping behind their fans.

"This way," Deborah murmured as she led them past the large desk in the center of the room.

She stopped before the door of a private lounge behind the staircase spiraling to the floor above. The room was small, affording only two settees with a table between them upon which already burned an oil lamp.

A large oil painting of a woman in a pink dress, reading a book by a fountain, took up a large portion of the facing wall. Nicholas raised a brow. The painting was obviously a fake, and an ill-painted one—but then, what else did one expect of a circulating library?

The door had no sooner clicked shut than Olivia grabbed Deborah's hands. "I am so sorry, Deborah. It's the *letter. I lost it.*"

"What do you mean?" Deborah asked faintly.

Olivia shook her hands. "I mean that I…I lost the letter."

"Lost it?" Deborah frowned, and then darted a glance at Nicholas. "But…he's here?"

Both women looked at him, both puzzled.

"Pardon?" he queried.

Deborah blanched and turned back to Olivia, this time taking Olivia by the hand. "You lost my letter?" she repeated faintly, turning white.

"I…forgot entirely about it. When I remembered, I looked for it everywhere. *Everywhere.* I couldn't find it."

Deborah burst into tears.

"What letter might this be?" Nicholas frowned.

Deborah threw herself into Olivia's arms and sobbed, "My confession. *Twelve* pages of *confession.*"

"Confession?" Olivia smoothed her cousin's hair back from her face.

"I was at my wit's end," Deborah wailed. "I did not mean to lie. I didn't think you would act on what I said about Nicholas, Olivia. I was just so ashamed. After all, who could believe I was intimate with the stable hand?"

Olivia froze. "What are you saying?"

At last. The sordid truth. Nicholas held still, lest Deborah become distracted and change her mind. Then, she slipped from Olivia's grasp and came up to him, pale and gliding like a ghost.

"Can you ever forgive me, Lord Blair?" she asked through white lips. "Can you forget that I lied and claimed you were the father? Can you forgive me?"

He'd embarked on the journey of solving Deborah's problems solely to impress Olivia, but now, as he looked into the poor lass's tortured eyes, he felt a deep sense of pity.

"Forgiven," he said at once.

If he'd thought she'd sobbed before, he was wrong. His words unleashed such a volley of tears that he excused himself from the lounge. Such matters were best settled between women. He adjusted his cravat and headed for the library door.

At last, the truth. At last, Olivia knew. He smiled and jogged down the stairs. When Deborah had calmed, he'd broach the matter of Lord Deveraux, and if his suspicions held true, he had no doubt that soon, he would see a genuine smile on the lass's face.

"Lord Blair?"

Nicholas looked over his shoulder and paused.

It was the Duke of Lennox. He didn't mind the man, as gruff as he was. However, the duke wasn't alone. At his side stood Lord Randall with a particularly smug smile on his infernal lips.

"Your Grace." Nicholas recovered to bow. He arched a brow and lowered his tone, "Randall."

Lord Randall spared him a nod. "Blair," he acknowledged before turning to the duke. "Then, Your Grace, if you will excuse me?"

"Tomorrow, then," the duke replied.

With a nod and an elegant bow, Lord Randall spun on his heel and took off down the street, swinging his silver-handled walking stick. Arrogance marked his every step.

Nicholas watched, displeased, until the man rounded the corner, out of sight.

"And?" The Duke of Lennox cut a formidable figure in his green kilt as he stood there, eyeing Nicholas from under his thick line of brows. "And?"

"Lord Randall, Your Grace." Nicholas drove directly to the point. "I would warn you to have a care with the man."

"What, exactly, are you insinuating, Blair?"

"Insinuating?" Nicholas met his gaze squarely. "No, I am warning, Your Grace. He is not what he appears."

The duke tilted his head to one side and a gleam entered his eye. "And you? Are you more than the rake you are known to be?"

Nicholas hesitated. Inexplicably, he wanted to be. Before he could answer, the duke's eyes latched over his shoulder in the direction of the library door.

"Grandfather?" Deborah's faint voice sounded behind him.

Nicholas turned to see Olivia standing beside her cousin on the top of the stairs. God, she was beautiful. Her color was high, and her breasts rose and fell as she locked gazes with her grandfather on the bottom step.

"Why did you not come to dinner, as summoned?" the duke challenged.

Olivia raised her chin and her eyes flared with passion. "I don't take kindly to orders."

The Duke's chin raised, in very much the same manner as Olivia's, and the stubborn expression crossing his face startled Nicholas almost into a snort of amusement. Olivia and her grandfather were so very much alike, from their posture, to the thinning of their lips, and down to the obstinate gleam in their eyes. The duke said nothing as Deborah descended the library stairs to join him. Reluctantly, Olivia followed.

When she arrived, the duke murmured, "This concert madness must stop, Olivia. You will be wed. Soon."

"Wed?" Nicholas blurted.

Neither Olivia nor the duke heard him.

Olivia graced the duke with a frozen smile of disdain. "I shall neither wed at your command, nor will I stop the production of *An Enchanted Summer Evening*, of that, I promise you. Now, I bid you good day." She turned away, then paused and turned back to Nicholas as if in an afterthought. "Good day, my lord."

Nicholas touched the brim of his hat. "Good day, Miss Mackenzie."

He watched her sweep down the street, his eyes again drawn to the mesmerizing sway of her hips.

"And?" the duke's voice grated.

Nicholas shifted his gaze to the man where he stood with Deborah by his side. "Your Grace?"

The duke's eyes narrowed perceptibly. "What are your intentions, Lord Blair? I see you often in the company of my granddaughter." He jerked his head at Olivia's rapidly disappearing form and added, "I speak of that one—not Deborah."

Deborah began to fidget. The poor lass. She reminded Nicholas of a nervous bird, a near hysterical one.

"Your intentions?" the Duke of Lennox repeated.

Intentions. Nicholas smiled. His intentions revolved entirely around Olivia wearing a ribbon and nothing else, but obviously, the duke wouldn't appreciate hearing such things. Clearly, there was only one thing he wished to hear.

To Nicholas's surprise, he heard himself saying, "Honorable."

Odd. The word was so much easier to say than he'd ever imagined, but then with Olivia, was it so curious a thing? Such women were meant to be courted for a lifetime—not just an affair.

"This is hardly a conversation for the streets of Glasgow." The duke scowled and folded his arms. "Though I will say that had you but spoken to me last week, I would have bidden you come to my library to discuss this matter. As it now stands, you are too late."

"Late?"

The duke lifted a grizzled brow. "Lord Randall has claimed her hand."

Nicholas snapped his head back. Good Lord above. Again. It was happening again. "*Never*," he spat.

He turned and strode away, nearly breaking into a run as he headed after Lord Randall. He found him near Salt Market Street, casually strolling with his blasted silver-handled walking stick still hooked over his arm.

"It's not happening, Randall," Nicholas announced as he arrived.

Lord Randall turned, surprised. "What madness is this?"

"You will never have Olivia," Nicholas grated. "Not this time."

The men locked gazes.

"Why is that?" Randall hissed.

Nicholas didn't hesitate. "Because I am."

NICHOLAS POURED ANOTHER WHISKY—HIS THIRD—AND PACED before the fire. It was late. He couldn't sleep. Not since his encounter with Randall that afternoon. Memories of the past haunted him. He wouldn't let Randall steal Olivia from under his nose as he had Henrietta. Nae, he'd visit Olivia in the morn-ing. There was nothing to stand in their way now that Deborah—

A sharp knock on his door proved to be Mr. Timms and his waistcoat. The blasted thing had popped another button since they'd last met.

"Come in." Nicholas stood aside.

"I came as soon as I could, my lord," the man huffed.

"I thank you." Nicholas nodded to the empty chair before the fire. "Whisky?"

"Please."

Nicholas waited until he'd settled the man before the fire,

drink in hand, before questioning, "Lord Randall? You have news?"

"Aye. The man teeters on the verge of ruin. Nae, he stands upon a precipice. He's desperate," Mr. Timms continued, withdrawing a sheet of paper from his waistcoat pocket. "The charities were swindles, my lord. He targeted lonely, wealthy women."

Nicholas's brows yanked up in surprise. "How long?"

"How long, my lord?"

"Lord Randall's bankruptcy? When did he fall into ruin?"

"It was his father that fell, my lord."

Nicholas blinked, surprised. A puzzle, indeed, and one many years in the making. So, it was Henrietta's wealth that had compelled the man to seduce and ruin her. His lack of emotion upon her death now made sense.

Again, there was a knock on his door. Nicholas looked at the clock. The hour was late. Near midnight. He heard her sultry voice before he saw her. She was speaking the instant the door began to open.

"I came the moment I received your letter, *mon amour.*"

Florinda Marie de Bussonne, the Lark of Paris. She stood before him, perfect, seductive—from the elaborate ringlets spilling over one shoulder to the soft white silk of an evening gown, caressing each curve in the most flattering way.

Nicholas smiled and stepped back, eyeing her appreciatively as she passed before him. She'd scarcely entered the room before she was slipping her arms around his neck to pull his head down for a kiss. Of course, he obliged, but the kiss was a chaste one. He stepped away.

Florinda's expressive brown eyes lit with interest. "Who is she?" She tilted her head to one side.

"Pardon?"

She smiled, a playful pout. "Only a Nicholas in love would kiss me so. A Nicholas *not* in love with me."

"Pardon, my lord," Mr. Timms cleared his throat, his face beet red. "Shall I be leaving?"

Nicholas grinned as Florinda's lips formed a perfect 'o.' "I thought you were alone," she murmured, and turned to the man. "Do not leave on my account, please."

"My business was done, madame," Mr. Timms assured as he clapped his hat onto his head. "My lord." He bowed.

Nicholas nodded in return. "Keep me informed of any further news, will you?"

"Aye, my lord," the man promised.

The next moment, Timms vanished down the darkened hallway and Nicholas shut the door.

"Nicholas." Florinda lowered her lashes.

"Olivia. Her name is Olivia." Nicholas chuckled.

Florinda's dark lashes fluttered and her pout deepened. "Then, it is this Olivia that has stolen you from me? For how long?"

Indeed. How long? Nicholas reached for the door, yet again. "I fear, it will be a long time, Florinda. Now that I think on the matter, 'tis best you stay elsewhere this night to prevent misunderstandings. Allow me to procure you a room."

He stepped into the hall, and as she followed, he offered her a gallant arm.

Florinda sighed. "How long is a 'long time,' dear Nicholas?"

There was only one true response to that question. He knew that now. "A lifetime."

CHAPTER 16

OLIVIA CLOSED HER EYES AND YAWNED. EXHAUSTION WEIGHED her every step, making her feel as if she were manacled to a ball and chain. She'd worked the night through. She yawned again. If only she could sleep.

Rubbing the back of her neck, she glanced around at the practically bare print room. There were only two pots of ink left and a half ream of paper, but she had five tidy stacks of music. Her father had even made several arrangements for flute and violin, as well as the piano.

She ran her hand over the smooth surface of the finished print. She'd always loved the smell of fresh ink on paper… Would all this come to an end soon? Four days. She had four days to delivered Mr. Pitt's final payment, along with proof of Louisa's return.

As for the concert? There were only two weeks left. As soon as she paid the fee, the musicians would expect to rehearse. The posters would go up in the hall. Tickets would be sold at the hall.

Olivia bit her lip. She'd yet to learn of Louisa's whereabouts or garner a response to her letters. It was as if the woman had vanished. Surely, *surely*, someone would find her? Give her the letter?

Good Lord, what would she do if she really didn't appear? A concert without a singer? What choice did she have? Louisa was the only singer she knew who could draw a crowd. The rest were unknowns. Singers of a higher caliber would scarcely work with the daughter of Glasgow's Mad Printer.

"Get to work, Olivia," she growled as she stalked back to her stool, sat down and reached for the rack of musical type.

Doubtless, Louisa was on her way back to Glasgow already. Where else would the woman earn such a handsome fee?

Grimly, Olivia selected the tiny iron-cast notes while her father's piano notes drifted through the room, an *adagio* of a particularly mournful quality that summoned tears.

She closed her eyes. She could never give up. Not only had she gone too far to turn back now, she could never betray her father in such a way.

No, the only path before her now was to believe Louisa would return.

Stifling yet another yawn, she squinted at the type, her eyes burning from exhaustion. Three staves left on the page and then, two pages more before she was done with the arrangement.

Dutifully, she lined the tiny rests and notes. Somewhere on the bottom of the second page, she caught herself nodding to sleep. With a yawn, she shoved the rack aside and, leaning forward, propped her head in her arms. She had to close her eyes—if only for a blessed minute. With a smile, she rubbed her nose on her sleeve and let her lashes droop.

She sat in the balcony box as the last strain of her father's music resounded in the hall. Below her, the crowd had risen to its feet. Brava. Brava.

"Olivia."

A hand touched her face. Olivia scowled and swatted the fingers away.

"You didn't print nearly enough, child," Mrs. Lambert was grinning over the heads of the crowds pressing into her shop. "Heavens, they're even lined out into the streets." She ran to the door. It was true. They lined as far as the eye could see...

"Olivia," the voice repeated, deepening.

Suddenly, Nicholas was there, kissing her again...

A thumb brushed her lips. She moaned, a panting kind of moan. Oh, how she'd missed his kiss. A groggy kind of awareness pierced Olivia's dreams and she stirred, opening her eyes. Nicholas. He stood there, his startling blue eyes mere inches from hers. She stared, simply smiling into them. Then, her confusion left her in a flash.

He really *was* there, and she was staring at him like a fool.

"This must be Miss Mackenzie?" a woman's angelic voice asked.

Olivia leaned back and glanced at the print room door. A beautiful woman stood just inside the print room. Dressed in a simple peach muslin with rosebud scalloped lace lining the collar and sleeves, she looked just as much the angel as she sounded.

Feeling suddenly inadequate, Olivia straightened, her hands instinctively lifting to smooth her hair. Lord help her, she must look a sight with ink-stained hands and a rat's nest of a hair. She suddenly became aware of a dampness on her chin. She cringed. Had she drooled in her sleep?

"May I introduce you?" Nicholas asked. "Olivia, this is Florinda Marie de Bussonne. Florinda, may I introduce Miss Olivia Mackenzie?"

Florinda. She hadn't met many of those. Why did the name sound familiar? Olivia frowned, but she shrugged the thought aside. If truth be told, she was more curious as to the nature of this Florinda's relationship with Nicholas. Obviously, she was precisely the kind of woman he'd fall for. Sophisticated. Exquisite. Were they lovers? Did she—

Olivia gasped as realization struck. "Florinda de Bussonne? The *Lark of Paris?*" She jumped to her feet.

Florinda didn't appear to notice. She was peering back over her shoulder. Turning on her heel, she abruptly left the print room.

Nicholas arched a curious brow. "Florinda?"

Puzzled, Olivia hurried to the door. The famed opera singer hadn't gone far. She'd paused at the parlor door, her finger to her lips, listening to the soft sounds of the piano within. Olivia held her breath as again, her father's mournful *adagio* filled the air around them. Finally, when the song finished, the woman turned to Olivia, tears glistening the corners of her eyes.

"*This* is the music? This? This is what you wish me to sing?"

Olivia held still, astonished. The *Lark of Paris* sing her father's songs? How could such a thing be?

"There is no question," Florinda said as she reached for the knob. "I *must* sing this. I *must* hear the rest."

"Wait." Olivia caught up to her in a single step.

The woman paused and lifted a perfectly sculpted brow.

"My father," Olivia whispered. "A carriage accident injured him sorely. He…he is unwell and interruptions upset him."

The opera singer's beautifully chiseled lips pursed in a line, and then she nodded. "Your father is an angel, Olivia. Only an angel can make music so beautiful." She turned to Nicholas and pointed to the door. "Nicholas, bring me a chair. I will sit here and not disturb this angel of music, but I *will* listen."

Nicholas? The familiarity rankled Olivia more than she could ever have imagined, and unaccountably irritated, she hurried toward the kitchen to fetch the chair herself. She should be dancing with joy that the famed Florinda would even *entertain* the notion of singing her father's songs—why could she only wonder if she slept in Nicholas's bed?

Scowling, she grabbed the back of the nearest chair.

"Are you upset?" Nicholas murmured.

So. He'd followed. Olivia pursed her lips and turned. He stood close, much closer than propriety should allow. His dark gray coat strained a little over his broad shoulders, the sight making her pulse skip a beat. Damn him. Why did he have to be so handsome? The crease in his cheeks deepened as he stood there, so very obviously aware of the effect he had on her.

"She is your lover." The accusation slipped from her lips.

His lashes dipped, betraying his surprise at the question, but then he chuckled. "Was. A long time ago. No more." He paused, then dropped his voice. "Dare I say, you're jealous?"

Were all men such fools as to state the obvious? "You are free to do as you please," she retorted. "It's no concern of mine how many women you dally with." She stepped forward, dragging the chair behind her.

He blocked her path, suddenly serious. "Nae, but it is your concern. I am no longer the man I used to be, I assure you. What matters of the past? What matters is how loyal I will be to the last woman I meet, is that not so? I assure you, I've no need nor desire to look elsewhere anymore."

The look in his eyes made her heart pound. She scowled. Her body certainly wasn't on her side. "If you'll excuse me, Lord Blair?"

She placed her palm flat on his chest to push him aside.

It was a mistake. The hard plane of his muscles beneath her fingers glued her hand in place and even through his waistcoat and shirt, she felt the heat of his skin. He drew a breath, a slow one, and a lazy look entered his eye. Olivia swallowed. He was going to kiss her again. She knew it. Her eyes dropped to his lips, appearing so hard, as if carved from stone, yet so velvety smooth at the same time.

"Nicholas?" Florinda's voice called from the hall.

Her angelic tones shattered the spell. Nicholas groaned in

disappointment as Olivia pushed him back and moved past him into the hall, dragging the chair behind her.

The opera singer's brown eyes were shining with emotion. "I beg you, Olivia, I *must* sing these songs. I, alone. Do not allow another, I beg you. It is *I* who must sing them first."

Olivia drew a sharp breath and shoved the chair in place against the wall. "As much as I would be honored—Nae, it would be a dream come true—I can't even *begin* to pay the fee for a singer of your fame—"

"Oh, please," Florinda interrupted, rolling her expressive eyes. "These songs will be forever tied to my name. I will become *historic*. I ask for little, I assure you. Indeed, I would sing them for no fee if I am given the exclusive rights to perform these songs for a year and a day."

Olivia cast a sidelong glance at Nicholas as he arrived. Had he paid the woman to say such wonderful words? Did she owe him again, in addition to the roof?

A sudden bang from the front of the shop caused them all to turn as one toward the curtains.

"Olivia? Olivia?"

The next moment, Deborah flew down the narrow hallway, her hair tumbling loose about her shoulders and her eyes wide with fear.

"What is it? Whatever is it?" Olivia gasped, rushing to meet her with hands outstretched.

"Whatever shall I do?" Deborah sobbed, her voice hysterical. She squeezed Olivia's hands tightly. "Blackmailed. I am being *blackmailed*."

"Blackmailed?" Olivia repeated, stunned. "Who?"

"I do not know," Deborah wailed.

She threw herself into Olivia's arms and burst into tears.

The piano in the parlor paused.

Olivia drew a breath. She couldn't have her father upset. Taking Deborah by the arm, she guided her into the kitchen.

They'd just stepped inside when the piano resumed. Olivia closed her eyes in relief. At least one crisis averted.

"What shall I do?" Deborah choked.

"Blackmailed? How?" Nicholas asked.

Olivia looked up. He'd followed them into the kitchen, his lean jaw tight and his eyes narrowed.

"The letter." Deborah wiped her face and turned to Nicholas. "Whoever it is, they have the letter."

The letter. Olivia winced. The accursed letter. Then, this was *her* fault, caused by her carelessness. The letter might have been sitting there for the week—who knew who could have taken it? "Forgive me, Deborah—"

"Oh, Olivia, who am I to judge another so harshly? How could it be your fault? It's my own. I am the one who ruined myself." Deborah burst into fresh sobs.

Nicholas reached over to grasp her shoulders and give them a little shake. "Now is the time to fight back, Deborah. Compose yourself, my dear. Tell me, what are the demands?"

After several attempts, Deborah managed to answer in a tremulous voice, "A letter. I received a letter, yesterday morning, and in it was the first page of my own handwriting. The letter claimed I had receive the rest of the pages if I left my mother's jewelry at the church." She choked, and added in a whisper, "I did. I took the jewelry there last night, just as I was told. This morning, I only got a single page of mine in return, along with a new demand, for more."

"Of course," Nicholas murmured. "You should have come to me first."

"How could I?" Deborah wept. "I was so ashamed."

She looked so lost, forlorn, that tears threatened Olivia's own eyes. "It's my fault," she repeated, hoarsely.

Neither Nicholas nor Deborah seemed to hear.

"May I see the demand, Deborah?" Nicholas asked. "Did you bring it?"

Deborah nodded and pulled at her reticule strings with shaking fingers. At last, she drew out a sheet of paper. "Two thousand pounds. In four days. They want me to bring two thousand pounds to the cemetery. Delivered by my own hand and no one else's."

Olivia simply stared. Two thousand pounds?

Nicholas's brows lifted in surprise.

"What shall I do?" Deborah whispered. "Grandfather will have to be told."

Silently, Nicholas scanned the letter, then, at last, looked up. "We will set a trap for this fool."

"How?" Deborah whispered faintly.

Nicholas folded the paper and tucked it into his waistcoat pocket. "Such a demand is preposterous. You'll leave him a letter in its place, demanding more time, arrange another meeting, what have you. It matters little. We'll catch this black-mailer at the cemetery, in the act."

A flash of hope crossed Deborah's face, then her face fell again. "It matters little, in the end. Either way, I am ruined. There is no denying this." She dropped her hand on her belly. "Soon, Grandfather will toss me onto the streets."

"Nonsense," Olivia objected. "He will do no such thing."

"Nae, he will," Deborah whispered.

"Then, you will come live with me," Olivia replied stoutly. Of course, she may soon be on the streets herself, but she couldn't think of that…not now.

"Oh, would you take me in?" Deborah squeezed Olivia's hand so tightly she winced in pain.

"There is another solution, is there not?" Nicholas inserted mildly. "Surely, you could speak with Lord Deveraux?"

Deborah's head jerked back as if she'd been slapped. "How do you know of him?"

"Does it matter?"

A series of emotions crossed her face, and then she turned her head to one side. "That ship has sailed for me, my lord."

"I happen to know he still cares for you," Nicholas disagreed in the gentlest of tones.

Wonder lit Deborah's face, but then her lips tugged down once again. She smoothed her hands over her rounding belly and whispered harshly, "Even if I cared, what man would accept a stable hand's child?"

"Perhaps, a man truly in love."

That made her humph, bitterly. "Nae, Lord Deveraux does not love me that much."

"I do believe, the question is do you still love him?" Nicholas asked, still insistent.

Fresh tears fell down her cheeks. She didn't need to speak the words.

Olivia frowned at Nicholas. Why torture the woman so? Clearly, Deborah still loved the man. "Enough," she hissed.

Nicholas eyed her, unperturbed, then turned back to Deborah. "Return home and write your response. I know a man who can catch this blackmailer in the act. Trust me, there is little to fear."

Deborah drew a wavering breath.

"As for your other matter." Nicholas dropped his eyes to her belly and smiled. "A week is all I ask. A week, and I do believe I can offer you a solution to your liking."

"A week?" Deborah whispered.

Olivia blinked, surprised.

With a broad smile, Nicholas held out his arm. "Shall I escort you to your carriage?"

Deborah darted a look at Olivia.

"Do go, Deborah." Olivia nodded.

"You are such a gentleman, Lord Blair," Deborah murmured as they stepped out of the kitchen.

As they vanished into the front of the shop, Florinda rose from her chair.

Doubtless, she'd heard. The shop was small, and they hadn't taken pains to speak softly, despite the music.

"Do pardon us—" Olivia began.

The opera singer smiled and put a finger to her lips. "Hush. It is an age-old story, is it not? I am the soul of discretion, my dear."

"Thank you." Olivia experienced another pang of jealousy. So, the woman was not only beautiful, but kind and honorable. Why did that bother her so?

"Miss Mackenzie," Florinda continued, her smile turning a shade rueful. "I know now is most likely not the best of times, but I am already late for a prior engagement. However, before I go, I have made up my mind."

"Pardon?" Olivia blinked.

"I beg you, draw up your contract and send it to my hotel. Allow me to take the music with me? I must practice, but there is enough time. We have two weeks, do we not? The musicians? Surely, you have hired them?"

The famed Lark of Paris…to sing her father's songs? Dare she hope?

"My dear, the musicians?" Florinda repeated.

"Yes," Olivia cleared her throat. "They were well known to my father, his friends. I gave them the music…months ago."

"Delightful." Florinda nodded. "Then allow me to take this music with me, so I can prepare."

In a daze, Olivia led her back to the print shop. Safe, in the cupboard, she'd stored the concert scores. She'd given one copy already to Louisa, but what did that matter now? Even if the woman appeared?

With growing excitement, but still unable to believe her luck, Olivia picked up the *An Enchanted Summer's Evening* score, returned to the singer and held it out.

"Nicholas asked you to sing, didn't he?" Olivia blurted. She hadn't known she was going to ask, yet now that she had, she wanted to know.

Florinda's eyes lit with a smile as she took the music reverently into her hands. "I owe Nicholas much, my dear," she murmured with a private smile. "I confess that I did jump at this chance to repay him, but now…now, after hearing your father's music, I fear I have only indebted myself to him all the more." She brought the score to her lips and kissed the cover. "Truly, your father is so talented, Olivia, but then…" she paused and looked her straight in the eye, "you know this already."

Olivia nodded, her throat closing with emotion. She could do little but stare and follow, rather like a lost duckling, as Florinda swept through the curtains and into the front of the shop.

"I must leave, Nicholas," she said as he stepped through the door. "I have so much to practice. The concert is soon. So very soon." She pushed past him, headed to the carriage waiting outside.

Nicholas grinned at Olivia and lifted a brow. "We need to speak, you and I."

Sudden shyness took Olivia by surprise. Rattled, she licked her lips and nodded, once.

Then, he strode off down the walkway toward the carriage.

She watched him through the window, allowing her gaze to linger on his broad shoulders, thighs and lean hips far longer than propriety allowed, but Lord help her, how could she resist?

Again, Nicholas had come to her aid. The roof. Her cousin. The opera singer.

Indeed, it seemed he was determined to solve her every problem. If only he could solve the ache in her heart, as well.

CHAPTER 17

"And where are you going?"

The rumble of Nicholas's deep voice made Olivia's heart leap with pleasure.

She paused on the path leading through Glasgow Green, composed herself and turned.

There he sat, astride a red roan a few yards away. The horse was a fine one, but the man on its back finer still. As she watched, he crossed one arm over the saddle and leaned forward with a lazy grin.

She was half-tempted to roll her eyes at herself. She was powerless against him, no different than any other woman in Glasgow. One look at those sea-blue eyes and her heart melted like salt in water.

Ah yes, she owed him an answer.

"Where am I going?" she repeated the question, primly lifting her chin as if she'd delayed her answer due to his mere impudence of asking. "If you *must* know, I am off to see Mr. Pitt."

Nicholas arched a sardonic brow, swung his long leg over

the saddle, and hopped down from his horse. "Why?" He stepped up to her side.

Would she ever get used to his height or the breadth of his shoulders? Olivia lowered her lashes, but there were just as many temptations below the waist as above. The way his tan breeches stretched over his strong thighs, for one. Dryly amused at herself, she forced her gaze back to his.

"Why else?" she repeated, resuming her walk. "To pay the man his money. Believe me, it most certainly is not a social call." Indeed, she'd dreaded facing the man alone.

"Allow me to accompany you, then," he suggested.

"Please." Olivia smiled. "I would be most grateful, I assure you."

His caught her hand and slid his thumb over her palm, slowly, languorously, before he looped her arm through his. She held her breath. His touch felt like fire.

"I haven't seen you…" She paused to clear the strangled sound from her voice. "I haven't seen you about these past few days."

"I had most urgent business in Edinburgh." He paused, then asked in a teasing tone, "Did you miss me?"

Heat rose to her cheeks and she turned her head away, praying he wouldn't notice. "Deborah has been fretting." She focused her gaze over the rolling lawns of Glasgow Green.

"She needn't fear," Nicholas assured.

"It's tonight, you know." Tonight, the blackmailer expected Deborah to bring the two thousand pounds.

"I assure you, Mr. Timms and his men stand at the ready. One of the men will be wearing her gown. We will catch the blackmailer in the act."

Olivia nodded. "I shall be so glad when this is over."

"We all will be," Nicholas agreed.

For a minute, perhaps more, they strolled side-by-side down the woodland path. The horse flicked its ears and snuffled as it followed.

Finally, Nicholas broke the silence with, "Are you attending the duke's dinner tomorrow evening?"

She hadn't wanted to, but Deborah had begged her to come. "Most reluctantly, on my grandfather's behalf," she confessed dryly. "But for Deborah, how can I deny her anything?"

Nicholas chuckled. "Your cousin is most fortunate to have you."

"I don't think so." Olivia sighed. "It is I who landed her in this mess."

"Hardly. Since I am also invited, allow me to escort you."

She glanced up, then nodded. He was behaving quite the gentleman. Why didn't he catch her about the waist and back her against an alley wall as he had their last meeting? Heavens, did he not *see* they stood near a forest?

"How goes the preparations for the concert?" he asked politely.

"Well. Very well." *Kiss me, Nicholas. Hard.* This time, she'd kiss him back, unfettered by a guilty conscience.

"And Florinda?"

The woman's name felt like a dash of cold water. "The woman has the voice of an angel," Olivia replied. "I heard her practicing when I arrived at her hotel with the contract."

"That is well, then."

Olivia faltered and then faced him. "You've done so much. The roof. Flor—"

"Hush," Nicholas murmured. He dropped the horse's reins to lay a finger on her lips.

The mere touch of his skin on hers made her want so very much. As if possessed, she parted her lips. Nicholas's expression altered. His lashes lowered, half covering his eyes. Then, slowly, he inserted his fingertip between her lips and over her tongue. Olivia held her breath.

"Soon," he said, his voice low, gruff, as he dropped his hand.

Soon? The word made her pulse leap.

Clearing his throat, he stepped back to retrieve his horse before offering his arm once again. "Mr. Pitt? How far?"

"Just over the bridge," she replied.

"Then, let us hurry. I am of a mind to indulge in other things far more pleasant than the company of Mr. Pitt."

Other things. Pleasant ones. Olivia drew a long, silent breath. She could hardly wait.

Mr. Pitt was displeased with both the money and Nicholas's presence by her side. It was clear he'd envisioned a far different ending to her predicament. Upon hearing the news that Florinda, the Lark of Paris, would be singing, he grinned, switching at once from lecher to a man of business.

"Well, this turned out fortunate, indeed," he said for the fourth time as he escorted them to the door. "*Most* fortunate. A wise investment. I knew you would surprise me. The Lark of Paris in the Theatre Royale." He wagged his head from side to side.

"The rehearsals start tomorrow," Nicholas announced.

"Indeed, my lord. Now we've a real concert here, I will have the lads prepare the stage right quick."

"See that all is ready," Nicholas continued.

"Indeed, my lord." Mr. Pitt bobbed up and down. "Indeed, I shall."

Olivia shook her head in wonder as they stepped out into the street. She cast a glance over her shoulder at the Theatre Royale rising so majestically behind her. In two weeks, Glasgow would finally hear her father's music.

Tingles of pleasure zipped down her spine.

She turned back to Nicholas. "The meeting with Mr. Pitt was far less trying than I feared. Thank you for coming."

He stood at her side, one corner of his mouth crooked. "My pleasure, I assure you." He caught her hand and brushed it against his lips.

The gesture reminded her of the 'other things' he'd promised. Her breath hitched.

"My carriage awaits." He squeezed her fingers.

Olivia blinked. "Your carriage?"

"I sent a messenger to fetch it whilst we concluded our business with Mr. Pitt." He drew her toward his coach-and-four, waiting under a nearby streetlamp.

After handing her inside, he seated himself opposite and then rapped the window.

As they began to move, Olivia smiled. "I should apologize."

Nicholas tilted his head to the side. "And why is that?"

"But then..." Olivia's smile deepened. "I find it strangely hard when I truly feel no need to seek forgiveness."

His brow furrowed in dry amusement. "For?"

"Writing the letter that summoned you." She never would have met him otherwise. "If I had known you were a man of character, perhaps I would have believed you from the start. But then, with a man of your reputation, what else is a woman to think?"

His blue eyes took on a gleam of amusement. "A man of my reputation?" In two swift jerks, he dragged the curtains across the carriage windows, then took a seat by her side.

Olivia lifted her chin. "Kiss me," she whispered.

The last syllable had barely left her lips before his mouth was on hers—at last. She opened to him at once, thrilling as his tongue danced over hers. She moaned, a wanton, yearning sound. She didn't care. She had nothing to hide, not anymore.

His hand lifted to cradle her neck as he deepened the kiss, then drew back, sucking her bottom lip as he pulled away.

"Must you return to the shop so quickly?" He peered down at her from mere inches away.

Olivia sighed. Pleasure would have to wait. "I am late already. I have enough to keep me busy for three days or more, honestly. There's still music to print and Father to mind while Mrs. Lambert runs errands of her own."

He said nothing but brushed the back of his hand over her cheek. A shiver of want rippled down the back of her neck. Again, his lips touched hers, lightly, but with an increasing fervor, and it was with a great sense of disappointment that she felt the carriage lurch to a stop.

With one last, light kiss, Nicholas lifted his head. "I shall return to escort you to the duke's dinner tomorrow. Shall we say, six o' clock?"

Olivia nodded.

After handing her down, he dropped a light kiss on her fingertips. "Tomorrow, then."

"I will be ready," she promised, then hurried into the shop.

It was a good thing Mrs. Lambert wasn't yet there. She wouldn't have failed to notice Olivia's kiss-swollen lips.

CHAPTER 18

NICHOLAS CAST HIS EYES TO THE SKY AND GAZED AT THE STARS covered by the occasional wisp of cloud. He'd left the hotel an hour ago, unable to sleep, and he wasn't aware he'd returned to Olivia's music shop until he stood several yards away from the faded sign.

Slowly, he folded his arms over the black iron railing of the fence and listened to the sounds of the piano drifting from the back window. Her father was a talented musician. There was little doubt the concert would be a smashing success, and even less that it would lift Olivia well out of her financial troubles. Most likely, she'd establish a fine reputation as a music publisher and a discoverer of talent, as well.

A figure moving in the shadows halfway down the street caught his eye. His lip quirked in a grin. He'd recognize the sway of those hips anywhere. He straightened.

The figure slowed. Then, Olivia's voice queried, "Lord Blair?"

"Why are you wandering the streets of Glasgow at such a late hour?" he asked in a lazy drawl.

She snorted, then arrived by his side. "I must work." She

tugged the fingers of her gloves to remove them. "I had music to deliver."

The thought of her delivering packages rankled him. "Do you not have a shop lad for such work?"

She gave a derisive chuckle. "The shop boys I can afford are useless. I must save every shilling I can. I have so much music yet to print." She took a step toward the door, then added, "Will you come inside?"

"I would be most delighted."

Once the shop door clicked shut behind them, Olivia asked, "Have you news of the blackmailer?" Her voice sounded loud in the darkened shop.

"We are ready." His eyes began to adjust to the darkness. "He shall not escape our net."

"That is good," she murmured as she moved past him.

"How goes the rehearsals?" He leaned his elbows on the counter.

"Florinda has the true voice of an angel." She paused, then added dryly, "But then, you know that."

"Truth be told, I haven't seen the woman in some years," he replied. "She could very well croak like a frog, now."

Olivia snorted faintly. She hung her hat and pelisse on a hook near the curtain, then returned to join him.

"It was you, wasn't it?" The moonlight lit her face as she tilted her chin upwards.

"Me?" he prompted with a curious brow.

"That day, in the shop. The day I was robbed. You sent Mr. Pitt on his merry way."

Nicholas chuckled and doffed his hat. "It was my pleasure, I assure you."

Olivia shook her head. "You have been prying into my business, Lord Blair. The matter of Mr. Pitt. The roof. Florinda."

The roof. He'd quite forgotten. "Where's the harm?"

She stepped around the counter. "I will repay you. With the

concert, I will finally establish myself as a music publishing house to be reckoned with."

Then, she was in his arms, melting into his embrace. The darkness only accentuated her softness. He smiled into her hair, the piano's melodic chords the only sounds heard as he passed his hands slowly over her hips.

How he longed to play her body, note by delicious note. He breathed deeply, inhaling her scent, and then slowly, savoring each blessed moment, bent his head and dropped his lips to the soft flesh of her neck.

Soft. So velvety soft. She drew a long breath, one that hitched at the end. The sound seemed to pass right through him, leaving a trail of fire in its wake. By God, how he wanted her. Intentions? Aye, he had honorable intentions. He'd wed her, of course. That didn't mean he couldn't indulge in a little delight of the senses now. Something she clearly wanted as much as he.

He shifted lower, kissing a trail to her collar bone. The moonlight filtering through the window lit her skin with a silvery glow, enough to contrast the flesh of her square collar line and the soft swells of her breasts pushing up, teasing him. Her lips found his. He kissed her back. She was so willing and warm. She moaned, instinctively pressing against him.

Heat thrummed through him, the kind of heat that could end with her beneath him, a ribbon tied beneath her naked breasts. It was too soon, of course, but, by God, he'd enjoy straddling the line. He traced his tongue under the seam of her lip, then drew back to graze her lips with his teeth.

She shivered, her breasts so soft against his chest. His hand lifted and caught the underside of that luscious curve. She arched against him, ever so slightly. Good God, she was a temptress. He drove his tongue into her mouth as he cupped his hand over her soft swell. This time, the moan was his. His cock hardened. It took every ounce of discipline he possessed to still his hips. How he ached to rock against her.

The piano played on, strains of a hauntingly beautiful melody, as she ran her hands up his chest. He shivered. She held him in the palm of her hand. Did she know just how much power she wielded?

He nuzzled the sensitive flesh beneath her ear and squeezed her breast as he dropped his free hand low over the base of her spine and down to the curve of her buttocks. She was so ripe. So luscious. His cock ached, straining his breeches. His blood began to pound. He needed more. He needed to taste her flesh, at least.

She moaned, shivering as he dropped a line of kisses over her collar bone. Then, he lifted his hand and pulled her gown down, over her shoulder. Her hard nipple rolled against his palm. She pressed against him. He smiled, and dropped his head further, planting kisses over her soft flesh as he lifted her breast to his eager lips.

"Heavens," she whispered as his mouth closed over her nipple.

As her hands threaded through his hair, he groaned with pleasure, drawing deep upon her.

"Nicholas," she panted.

Her gown dropped off her other shoulder, baring both breasts to his touch, his mouth. He switched breasts, teasing her nipple with his teeth as he lightly pinched the one he'd just released. She gasped and arched her hips against him. His thinking slowed...was there even thinking involved, anymore? —beyond that of sliding his cock into the sweet heat between her legs? He nursed upon her, nipping and suckling as she dropped her head back, exposing the long line of her white, tender neck.

By God, he was tempted to take her, right there. He kissed his way back up to her mouth, his cock hard, the buttons on his breeches threatening to burst. He noticed the piano had fallen silent and footsteps approached.

"Olivia?" her father's voice called out.

With a quirk of his lips, he chuckled under his breath, stepped back, and quickly drew her gown over her shoulders. She caught her breath and cast a look to the curtains.

"Tomorrow," he whispered in her ear.

Tomorrow, he'd escort her to the duke's dinner…and after?

He smiled as he slipped out the front door, making his escape as her father entered the shop. He was halfway down the lane before he realized he'd left his hat behind.

CHAPTER 19

Nicholas arrived an hour early. He entered the shop resplendent in gray breeches with a brocade waistcoat of a darker hue. His red silk cravat only made his eyes look all the more blue.

"Five shillings, Miss Park." Olivia tossed Nicholas a smile, then handed the bundle of music to the young woman. "Thank you for coming."

The young woman set the coins down. "Why, thank *you*, Miss Mackenzie. The parson's wife has been singing your praises. So modestly priced and for such a wonderful selection and quality."

Olivia smiled again. "Thank you. I hope to see you again."

"Most assuredly." Miss Park took up her bundle and turned for the door.

Olivia nearly snorted aloud the way the young woman's shoulders stiffened. She'd obviously caught sight of Nicholas.

In dry amusement, Olivia watched her bounce his way.

"Allow me." With a polite dip of his chin, Nicholas opened the door and stood aside.

"Why, thank you, kind sir," the young woman tittered.

Olivia folded her arms and leaned against the counter. The young woman began to fuss with her package, then paused to check her gloves. It was the adjustment of the hat that prevented her from leaving. Olivia's amusement deepened. Just how many ways could a woman slow her exit through a door? Now, it was back to the hat, adjusting the brim. Surely, the sun wasn't that deadly?

Finally, Miss Park stepped forward, but no more than three inches from the threshold, she paused to bestow her most dazzling smile on the man still waiting patiently for her to leave.

Olivia faked a yawn.

Nicholas's eyes latched onto hers with some amusement. Obviously, he was used to such antics. *Good God, the woman was now checking her shoe?* Did she think it had disappeared...ah, of course...she sought to provide him a flash of ankle. Unfortunately, the effort was a wasted one. Nicholas was still smiling at Olivia and failed to notice.

"Miss Mackenzie," he called across the shop with a wink, "my carriage awaits your pleasure."

With a huff, Miss Park stepped outside.

When the door closed, Olivia laughed. "I will take it kindly if you don't offend my customers, Lord Blair."

"How so?" he asked with a chuckle.

Olivia watched him saunter to the counter. She couldn't blame the poor lass. He was a handsome specimen. "You missed the ankle. She worked so hard to offer you a glimpse."

Nicholas leaned down and crossed his arms on the counter, positioning his forearms so that their elbows touched.

Olivia drew a deep breath.

"It's not *her* ankle I wish to see," he murmured. "As you well know."

Olivia lifted her head as he tilted his, but he didn't kiss her. Instead, he stayed there, peering down at her through half-closed eyes, only inches away. The simple act fired a longing deep inside her. She wanted him. Lord, *how* she wanted the man. Still, she couldn't let him know just how much power he wielded. He thought to tease her? She could do the same.

With a smile, she removed her arms from the counter and stepped back. "You are early, Lord Blair."

"Am I?"

"I have yet to dress for the evening." She'd washed the ink out of her best dress just that morning. Hopefully, the summer heat had dried the thing.

"I will wait." He straightened. "Shall I mind the shop?"

The thought summoned a smile to her lips. "If word of that gets on the streets of Glasgow, I will have a mob of maidens at my door."

Nicholas laughed, then grew serious. "It is you I fret over. Once this concert of yours reveals your father's music, there will be more than Lord Randall sniffing here."

Lord Randall. Olivia grimaced. "I know how to handle the likes of Lord Randall."

"He's a crafty man," Nicholas countered. The muscle on his jaw twitched.

"He's a fool," she retorted. "Any man who thinks he will come by my hand by conspiring with my grandfather is a fool of the highest order."

She turned away, but Nicholas caught her elbow. She glanced back. The look in his eyes made her heart skip a beat. She watched, mesmerized, as he skimmed his palm lightly down her arm to slide his hand over hers. Lacing their fingers, he slowly brought her fingertips to his lips, his eyes locked with hers all the while.

"Then let the fool conspire away." He dropped a kiss on the tip of each finger. "I shall consult with the lady herself."

Olivia swallowed, a pit of want burgeoning deep inside her.

"I must ready myself," she finally said, her voice suddenly hoarse.

"Aye." He let her hand slip free, and added, "We shall continue. Later."

She hurried through the curtains and up the stairs. Later. Continue later? She could only hope so.

In the heat of her attic room, the dress had dried, all but the hem. She took her time changing, mostly to regain control of the thoughts he'd unleashed. It was difficult. Memories of his lips on her breast kept rising in her mind, trampling all others.

Of course, she was engaging in the utmost of scandalous behaviors, and, of course, she should wed before she let a man touch her so...but, strangely, she didn't care. It was Nicholas she wanted. She had from the very moment she'd met him.

She eyed her reflection in the mirror. Of course, they could never wed. He was far above her station. Her choices lay in men such as Timothy. She shuddered at the thought of him touching her, suckling as Nicholas had. After Nicholas, how could she give herself to another man? She would rather have him and become his mistress than not at all.

"Enough, Olivia," she informed her reflection as she fanned her cheeks.

Enough, indeed. She had Deborah to succor first, a wrong to be righted.

She reached for her hat and pelisse from the bed. It was time to go and support her cousin. Doubtless, worry over the blackmailer was eating her alive.

"I assure you, all is in order. Mr. Timms will trap the man," Nicholas said. "Trust me, Olivia."

Olivia nodded. "I do."

He lifted the brass knocker on the Duke of Lennox's town-house door and knocked three times.

Three hours. In three hours' time, the blackmailer would be waiting for Deborah to hand over two thousand pounds. Knowing her cousin as she did, she figured she must be on the verge of fainting from stress.

She was.

As the maid ushered Olivia and Nicholas into the drawing room, Deborah rose from the settee looking pale, wan, and definitely most ready to collapse.

"Deborah, my dear." Olivia rushed to her side.

"Olivia. Nicholas," she choked in greeting.

She opened her lips to speak, but clamped them shut as the Duke of Lennox chose that moment to arrive.

"Blair," the man grunted with a curt nod, then he turned his censorious gaze upon Olivia. "Are you still continuing this madness at the Theatre Royale?"

"And a good day to *you*," Olivia snapped. Eyes locked with his, she opened her reticule, withdrew a slip of paper, and held out her hand. "A gift. For you."

Wordlessly, he accepted the offering with a frown.

Olivia graced him with a frosty smile. "It's your ticket to *An Enchanted Summer Evening*."

The duke's brows yanked upwards.

Deborah squeaked.

"Impudent chit." He crumpled the ticket in his hand.

"You're welcome." Olivia lifted her chin.

The duke eyed her for several long moments and then abruptly turned away.

As he strode toward the hearth along the opposite wall, Nicholas suddenly laughed.

The sound made them all jerk in surprise.

"Come in, lad." Nicholas held out his hand in greeting

toward a figure in the doorway. "I am glad you made it, after all."

The man stepped into the room, a tall, lean fellow with a hawk nose and dark, shoulder-length hair. Olivia had no time to notice anything else as Deborah suddenly choked at her side, and then sucked in a huge gasp of air.

"What is it?" Olivia asked, all at once alarmed.

Deborah stared straight ahead, stricken.

"May I introduce Lord Deveraux, Your Grace?" Nicholas nodded at the duke where he stood by the fire.

Lord Deveraux bowed in respect. Olivia frowned. Lord Deveraux? The name sounded quite familiar. *Good lord. The man Deborah loved.*

"I cannot," Deborah whispered, rooted to the spot.

"Ah, then you've decided," the duke grunted. He nodded his chin at Deborah.

Lord Deveraux turned. "Please, Deborah. We must speak."

Deborah stared as if he were a ghost. As he took a step toward her, she bolted from the room with Lord Deveraux on her heels.

"What the devil?" the duke bellowed.

Grumbling, he turned back to the fire, but he'd no more than done so when Lord Randall appeared in the doorway.

"Good evening," Lord Randall's voice slithered into the room.

Nicholas shifted, the line of his shoulders at once rigid.

"Randall." The duke didn't look at the man.

"Good evening, Your Grace," Lord Randall saod. His eyes drifted over Nicholas and then latched onto Olivia's. "Miss Mackenzie, 'tis a pleasure to see you, again."

Olivia looked up. Why wouldn't the man simply leave her be? "Lord Randall," she acknowledged with the barest of civil replies.

Lord Randall glanced back at Nicholas. Neither spoke, but the tension between them pulsed.

The dinner bell chimed.

The duke stirred.

Olivia waited, pensive.

"Randall, a word." Nicholas pointed to the door.

Lord Randall hesitated, then nodded with obvious reluctance.

As the two men passed into the hall, the duke scowled. "Will no one respect the dinner hour?"

Olivia smiled. "Shall we retire to dinner?"

Her grandfather cocked his head to the side. "You would dine with me, alone?"

"I do not fear you," Olivia replied with a shrug. "And I must admit, I am hungry. I have been up since dawn. Why waste a good meal?"

Her grandfather held out his arm in escort. Ignoring him, Olivia sailed down the hallway and into the dining room.

The dining room décor was gloomy, at once reminding Olivia of her grandfather. A grandfather clock ticked in the corner and a portrait hung over the fireplace. Beyond that, there was little to offer cheer in the dismal room.

The table had been set for six. Ignoring the spidery writing indicating she should sit on her grandfather's right with Lord Randall by her side, Olivia walked to the foot of the table and took the seat opposite her grandfather at the head.

The duke sat down. "You are accustomed to having your way." It was a clear criticism.

Olivia shrugged. "No more than you, I am sure."

Her grandfather scowled. "I am the head of my house. I have earned such respect. You are in sore need of a husband to guide your ways."

She spared him a look of disdain. "I will allow none to meddle in my concerns. Least of all, you. I will never wed Lord

Randall." She might as well drive to the heart of the conversation and get it done with, once and for all.

The old man's eyes took on a sharp gleam. "And if he can offer you a title?"

"You speak as if a title is the only treasure in the world," she observed.

"A title grants power. Respect."

"Nae, it does not." Olivia afforded a small laugh. "Both power and respect must be earned, and I am of the mind that a marriage should be founded on love."

The duke snorted in disdain. "Foolishness."

"Hardly."

"Lord Randall would offer you security, a—"

"Then let him offer such to another. My affections are already taken."

The duke scowled. "Who? Lord Blair?"

He was perceptive. She had to grant him that much, but then, true attraction to another was impossible to hide. Olivia lifted her chin. She wasn't her grandfather's puppet. She didn't have to answer him if she wished not to. She glanced at the portrait hanging over the fireplace, an oil of a young red-haired man with a drooping mustache, his mouth and brows angled in overt disapproval.

"My father," the duke said.

"I see the resemblance," Olivia muttered.

His brow arched. Clearly, in the physical respect, he couldn't be more opposite than the man glaring down at him, but there was no denying the family resemblance in disdain and arrogance. Olivia shrugged, not feeling compelled to explain.

The servants entered with a platter of quail with asparagus and orange jellies. When they'd finished serving, the duke waved them away.

As the man glowered at his plate, Olivia queried, "Have you

seen Lady Blair lately?"

The duke looked up, clearly surprised she'd dare break his governing silence.

She smiled, pleased she had. "I have been amiss in visiting her, of late."

A gleam entered the old man's eye, a gleam she couldn't quite place, but one that irritated her even though she couldn't place why. Was it a challenge?

As if possessed by some devil, she said, "I do so wish to consult with her. I have been mulling the idea of taking a portion of the proceeds of this concert and financing another in London." She hadn't, but now that she thought on the matter, it was an excellent idea.

The duke's head snapped back.

A *most* excellent idea. "And perhaps on to Paris," she continued, pleased.

"Have you no shame?"

"Odd." Olivia slowly set down her spoon. "That is a question I believe you should be answering rather than asking."

Again, to her surprise, the duke's eyes gleamed.

A movement near the door caused them both to turn as Nicholas strolled into the room, his cravat hanging slightly to one side and with a cut gracing his chin.

"Forgive my late arrival," he said with an easy grin.

Olivia smiled. "Lord Randall?"

"An unexpected emergency called him away." Nicholas took a seat in the middle of the table.

The duke peered at him from under drawn brows but said nothing. Olivia didn't mind. With Nicholas in the room, the conversation took a happier turn, and for the remainder of the meal, she found herself quite forgetting the duke altogether.

Finally, after the last course had been served with still no Deborah or Lord Deveraux in sight, the duke turned to Nicholas.

"The library?" he grunted.

Nicholas's lip quirked. "Surely, it is a crime to leave Olivia unattended in the drawing room?"

Olivia let her gaze linger on his mouth. Such a sensual mouth. She couldn't wait to feel his lips on her skin again.

"You well earn your reputation, Blair," the duke commented dryly.

Feeling her cheeks heat, Olivia rose from her chair.

The men followed suit.

"Then we shall break convention, and all retire to the drawing room," the duke snapped. "No doubt, Deborah is there already. I expect to hear welcome news."

His words puzzled Olivia as they headed toward the drawing room once again, but she said nothing.

Deborah *was* there, seated on the settee, her face aglow. Lord Deveraux sat by her side, holding her hand in his and speaking softly. As they entered, both Deborah and Lord Deveraux rose.

"And?" the duke prompted, stalking back toward the fireplace.

Lord Deveraux turned toward Deborah with a smile. "I am pleased to announce, Deborah has given me the honor of becoming my wife."

Olivia could only stare. Surely, the man knew she expected a child? He *had* to. Deborah looked so relaxed.

"Come, Olivia," Deborah hurried toward her, beaming from ear to ear. "I have a gift for you." She turned to the men in the room. "We shall return in but a few minutes."

"Allow me, first, to offer my congratulations," Nicholas stepped forward to catch Deborah's hand.

"I can never thank you enough, Lord Blair," Deborah whispered as he politely kissed her hand. "Frankly, I owe you my life."

Olivia turned to him in wonder. So, he'd solved Deborah's

problem, as well?

Deborah pulled her out of the drawing room and up the stairs to her bedroom.

"I can't believe it, Olivia." Her cousin's eyes shone as she shut the door and leaned against it. "Lord Deveraux has returned. He still loves me."

"I…I am so happy for you," Olivia whispered.

As if possessed by some devil, her eyes dropped to Deborah's expanding waist before she caught herself and quickly yanked them away.

"We are to be wed next week." Deborah closed her eyes. "Then, we will be off to the continent for a year."

A year. That was good. Enough time to have the child.

Deborah dropped her hand on her belly and gave it a pat. "We will say we adopted the child from his cousin, an untimely death of some kind. It's better for all, that way. After all, he can scarcely turn his estate over to…well, a child that is not of his blood. Still, he promised to love the child, as a child of mine."

Olivia nodded. Of all outcomes, this was the best she could hope for.

With a sigh, Deborah glided across the room to her bed and picked up a large box there, tied with green ribbon.

"This is for you." Deborah smiled.

"Me?"

Olivia joined her at the bed and untied the ribbon to pull back the brown paper and lift the lid. A dress lay there, a creation of gold silk. With a gasp, she held it up.

"It's for your concert," Deborah laughed shyly. "I had my dressmaker fashion it, of course, but I stitched the bodice myself."

Olivia ran her fingers over the finely stitched roses adorning the collar and trailing to the waist. Never had she owned so fine a thing. Her cousin's exquisite work brought tears to her eyes.

"It is beautiful," she whispered. "How can I thank you?"

"There's nothing to thank," Deborah smiled, misty-eyed. "I am grateful, for all of your help."

Olivia winced. "I have caused you more pain than help, I fear."

"Well, no more trouble than I caused myself," her cousin confessed with a nervous laugh.

They both laughed, a desperate kind of laughter.

The chiming of the downstairs clock announced the nine o' clock hour.

As one, they exchanged worried looks.

The hour of the blackmailer.

Olivia returned the dress to the box and replaced the lid. "Do not t fret, Deborah. Nicholas will handle the matter."

Deborah nodded. "You trust him so."

Trust him. Olivia smiled. She did—and more. Unbidden, a memory of his mouth on her breast summoned heat to her cheeks.

Deborah tilted her head speculatively. "So, it's that way between the two of you?"

Suddenly shy, Olivia nodded. Once.

Deborah smiled. "I am happy for you, Olivia."

"It's…it's not like we're engaged, Deborah." She bit her bottom lip. "Such a thing could never be."

"I understand." Deborah sighed. "Come. We must join the others."

They descended the stairs and returned to the drawing room once more, but it wasn't long before Olivia rose from the settee and approached Nicholas.

"I must be going," she said. "Mrs. Lambert cannot stay past ten."

"I will have the carriage brought, at once." His cheeks creased with a smile.

The expression in his eyes reminded her at once of his

earlier comment. She couldn't help but smile in anticipation.

Farewells were said. The duke grunted and retired to his private study, but Deborah and Lord Deveraux followed them outside and stood on the steps.

"Good night, Olivia." Deborah enveloped her in a hug and whispered, "How can I be so happy and yet so worried at the same time?"

"There's naught to fret over," Olivia assured. She turned to Lord Deveraux. "It's a pleasure to meet you, my lord."

"The pleasure is mine, Miss Mackenzie." He kissed her hand. "We shall speak again. Soon."

Nicholas escorted her to the carriage and handed her inside.

Olivia smiled, pleased with Deborah's outcome, and glanced out the window as the carriage dipped under Nicholas's weight. A shadowed figure stood directly across the street, under the trees. Was it a man? A shiver raced down her spine.

"I say, are those two kissing in the eyes of everyone?" Nicholas chuckled.

Olivia glanced through the open carriage door. Lord Deveraux and Deborah stood on the steps, locked in a kiss.

"Good Lord," he continued in mock disdain. "They will have to wed, immediately. Especially after that scandalous display."

He closed the door and the carriage began to roll.

"You did that," Olivia said with a prim smile. "You arranged her marriage."

She could sense him grinning in the darkness. "Nae, they arranged it betwixt themselves. I merely put them in touch, once again."

"Must you always solve others' problems?"

"I must admit, I am taking a liking to it," he replied easily.

For a time, the banter continued and then a pleasant silence fell. To Olivia's disappointment, he didn't sit by her side but remained in his seat. By the time she arrived at her door, she discovered that to have been a good thing. No doubt, he would have gotten her overly heated and wanting more, but from the looks of the shop, she hadn't the time for such distractions. Every window was lit. Even from the street, she could hear her father's voice. Quickly, Olivia hurried inside. Her father stood by the shelves, searching through the music.

"Lordy, Olivia," Mrs. Lambert heaved a sigh of relief. "Am I glad to see you, lass. He's been nigh on a handful this past hour, looking for his music."

"I have lost the score, Olivia," her father turned to her, visibly upset and his hat askew.

"What score?" Olivia asked in soothing tones, hurrying to loop her arm through his.

Her father focused his gaze over her shoulder. "And you? Who are you?"

Olivia glanced back. Nicholas had followed to stand by the door.

"I am Lord Nicholas Blair." He bowied. "I am at your service."

Her father drew his brows into a scowl. "State your intentions with my daughter."

Olivia blinked, surprised by his bluntness.

"The most honorable, I assure you, Mr. Mackenzie," came Nicholas's reply.

It was a lie, of course. There was no wedding in their future, but Olivia's heart quickened just the same.

She felt her father relax, then he gazed into her eyes, his clarity again gone. "My how you've grown, child."

"Come, father, it's time to rest." She began drawing him toward the curtains.

"Yes, yes, rest," her father murmured. Then, he glanced at Nicholas. "Good evening, Lord Blair."

"Good evening," Nicholas replied, hat in hand.

"I will be on my way," Mrs. Lambert said. "If you'll see me out, Lord Blair?"

"Most certainly, Mrs. Lambert." He offered a gallant arm. "A good evening to you, Miss Mackenzie."

Olivia smiled her farewell. It was a disappointment, truly. She'd envisioned such a different ending to the day, but not with her father in such a state.

"Come, father." She drew him behind the curtain and toward his room. "Shall I read to you?"

"No, no," her father yawned. "I am rather tired, my child."

"Then, this way, Father dear."

She guided him to his room and settled him into bed. To her surprise, he fell asleep almost at once. Olivia poked her head back through the curtain only to see the shop lying still, silent. With Mrs. Lambert gone, it was most unfortunate that Nicholas had left when he had. With a sigh, she ascended the stairs to her room and began to undress.

She might as well work, she still had music to print, but work was a sore substitute when she wanted Nicholas's mouth on her, suckling her breast and more. For the first time, she understood the pull of attraction, the desire to abandon everything for the love of a man. Love. Did she love Nicholas? She already knew the answer. She'd battled that attraction from the very start.

Quickly, she shimmied out of her gown and shift, then took her father's printing clothes from the clothing chest and slipped them on. She was too agitated to sleep. She might as well put the time and energy to use.

Forcing all thoughts of Nicholas from her mind, she left her room and returned to the floor below. The night was a hot one and the work of pulling the Devil's Tail, forcing sheet after sheet over the type, would make it hotter still.

Already, the print room was stuffy. She lit the candle on the counter and another on the press before heading to the windows to open the shutters. The cool night air would chase away the stuffiness. It was risky, of course. She'd have to keep watch to ensure Mr. Peppers didn't slip through to wreak havoc with his paws.

A cricket sang in the alleyway as she returned to the press and unbuttoned the top two buttons of her father's linen shirt. She grinned. She was half tempted to divest herself of clothing altogether. What did it matter? There was no one here to see.

She loosened her belt a notch, letting the breeches slide lower over her hips and then tied the shirt tails above her waist. Cool air kissed her skin. She sighed in relief and reached for the handle. She started. Nicholas lounged against the door-frame and watched her under heavily lidded eyes.

"How did you get in here?" she demanded in a voice that was far too breathless.

He grinned and unfolded his arms. "I never left."

It was impossible not to smile.

"Forgive me for interrupting," he murmured as he joined her.

Olivia drew a deep breath. Yes. He was close, as he should be. "Forgive you?" She peered up at him through her lashes. "Perhaps, I shall consider it."

"Perhaps?" He grinned and, leaning back, snuffed the candle on the counter with the palm of his hand, then blew out the one on the press.

Darkness filled the room.

Olivia's heart began to pound.

"Perhaps there is a way I can convince you to think positively in my favor," his deep voice whispered in her ear.

There were so many things he could do—that she *wanted* him to do.

Moonlight streamed through the windows, bathing the room in silvery light, enough so that she could see the outline of his smiling lips.

"You are so beautiful, Olivia."

That brought a laugh to her lips. "In the darkness only," she teased. "I am untidy, wearing breeches—"

"I rather think all women should wear breeches," he interrupted, placing a hand on the press behind her and stepping forward to press his body against hers.

Yes. That's what she wanted. To feel him, every inch. "Women wear breeches? Would it not be rather confusing to tell them apart from men?"

Nicholas lifted a wicked brow. "I rather think not. The shapes, I assure you, are decidedly different. There are advantages to such attire, I might point out."

The seductive purr in his voice made her heart sing. "Advantages? Pray tell?"

He ran a palm down the front of her shirt, lazily, the replied, "To begin with, the shirt. It's much easier to…open."

Her spine arched expectantly at the word. His mouth covered hers in a quick, deep kiss, one that made her instinctively tuck her legs together. As quickly as his lips had found hers, they drew back. He caught the bottom of her shirt and slowly slipped his hand beneath the hem.

As far as rakish behavior went, this was a prime example, of course, but she only willed his hand to slide up faster. She wanted his fingers on her breasts. Nae, she wanted his mouth.

Then, sweet heaven, his fingers found her nipple. "You're not wearing anything else beneath?" His lips curved into an expectant smile. He caught her nipple between his fingers and tugged.

A tingle of pleasure shot straight down to her belly. "Yes," she moaned.

He pressed her harder against the press, kneading her breast in his strong hand.

"Suckle me," she whispered.

"With pleasure," he answered, at once.

The next instant, he caught her bottom lip between his teeth as he removed his hand from her breast. She would have complained, but how could one talk with her lip being sucked?

He tugged the buttons of her shirt. They slipped free and the cloth fell away. Both of his hands returned to her breasts, and she gasped into his mouth, arching her belly against him. His mouth left her lips and kissed a trail over her jaw and down her neck, his fingers teasing her nipples all the while. She couldn't seem to hold still. Wetness pooled between her thighs and her muscles clenched.

Finally, his mouth moved lower until he was where she wanted him to be, lifting her left breast into his mouth. She gasped at the sensations of his hot, wet tongue circling her nipple. He began to suck, each tug sending a spike of sensation deep into her core.

"Nicholas. Yes. Oh, Nicholas."

She buried her fingers in his hair, pressing his mouth down harder on her breast as he suckled, taking her deeply. Dimly, she was aware of the tug at the belt holding her pants in place. She scarcely noticed. How could she, with the sensations his mouth evoked? Her pants fell to the floor, and as the cool air caressed her naked thighs, she lifted her lashes in shock. She was naked. His mouth left her breast and the trail of kisses resumed, down a straight line of her belly to continue lower.

Good Lord, he was kneeling between her legs. She froze, as he ran his fingers down the length of her legs, and then up again, his thumb sliding along her inner thighs.

"Open your legs for me," he murmured.

As if in a dream, she complied, mesmerized by the dim shadowy form kneeling between her legs. He caught her inner thigh in his hand and lifted her leg higher, pressing her back against the press as he draped her calf over his shoulder.

Then, he buried his face in her privates.

CHAPTER 20

NICHOLAS ACHED. BY GOD, HOW HE ACHED. HE HADN'T BEEN this hard since—well, he couldn't recall—and there would be little relief ahead for him. He couldn't take her. Not standing up against the press. Not her first time. He had to teach her the joys of her body first.

Not that he wasn't enjoying himself. He was. Immensely. He guided her leg up and out, enough to grant him access to what he wanted. The sight of her legs opening for him, revealing the shadows of her nether lips nearly made him spill his seed. Then, he tasted her, slid his tongue between her crease as she arched in shock, then delight.

Clearly, no man had ever tasted her flesh. The knowledge filled him with a sense of pride, of ownership. She was his and his alone. His tongue found her swollen nub. He paused to tease her with his tongue and then continued to lick in long, slow strokes, from the base of her channel to her tight little pleasure bud.

She began to move. He smiled. He would make her sing as the musical instrument she was. Carefully, he slid the tip of his finger into her channel. By God, she was wet for him. He continued the slow torture of licking her folds. Again, he inserted his finger and drew it out, establishing a rhythm in time with the thrusting of her hips.

She moved faster, hanging onto the press as if her life depended upon it, her breasts swinging as she pushed herself against his face. It was too much. Blood rushed to his cock, turning him marble hard. He unbuttoned his breeches, allowing his shaft to spring free and dropped a fist over its length. His hand was a poor replacement for her channel, but she couldn't take him. Not yet. Synchronizing the movement of his fist with the thrust of her hips, he returned to teasing her with his tongue.

She groaned and began to pant, the soft sounds driving him to near madness. She needed more. He knew that. He wanted so much to rise to his feet and thrust his pulsating shaft deep into her channel and truly make her his. How he wanted to spill his seed deep inside her as they both shrieked with pleasure.

Instead, he quickened the speed of his hands, on himself and her as well and swirled his tongue around her pleasure bud. Her hands dropped to his head. Her fingers anchored into his hair as her hips arched. She turned into a mad thing desperate for release. Then, her release came.

She looked so beautiful, naked, writhing on his hand, her lips parted. Her body spasmed around his fingers, under his tongue, as his cock hardened to the point of pain.

She let out a shriek. There was no faking the pleasure that swept over her. This was nothing like Demelza's false pleasures or even Florinda's well-practiced gasps. Olivia's pleasure burst out raw, real. She quivered, her body clenching around his fingers as she hung onto the press, desperately. The sight was too much. His own pleasure took him by surprise, both in speed and strength. A grunt tore from his chest as he released his seed.

As their pleasure passed, he remained kneeling between her legs, enveloped by her musky sent. As the intimacy of what had just passed between them threatened to make him hard again, he buttoned up his breeches and pushed to his feet.

"Marry me." He took her in his arms.

"Pardon?" she gasped.

"Marry me," he said again, louder.

She straightened. "I can hardly marry you."

"Why?"

"Come, now. You're a lord. I am—"

"Beautiful," he cut in to finish her sentence. "Loving. Warm. Brilliant. So very smart and driven."

She smiled, then somehow, slipped free of his grasp. Quickly, she gathered her clothes from the floor and began to dress. "You certainly do own your reputation, Lord Blair."

Nicholas lifted a brow. "That's a strange response to a man who just asked you to wed him." He wanted no other. He knew he never would.

"Enough teasing," she admonished. "You have me, Lord Blair. Good Lord, you have me. How can I tell you no? I want to be in your bed surely as much as you want me there."

He grinned. Her answer was as good as a yes.

"Now, be gone. I have work to do."

Nicholas chuckled. "Then, my dear, let us begin."

Nicholas stretched and opened his eyes. For a moment, he stared at the ceiling above in confusion. Rough-hewn rafters, aged and weathered by time. Then, the smell of ink summoned memories. Olivia's print room. He'd stayed the night and had helped her finish printing the music. They had have finished much earlier if they'd been able to keep their hands off each other.

He grinned.

He'd licked her again as they'd laid on the floor together. She lost herself to the throes of passion. Never had he seen such a beautiful sight. He had almost made her his. Almost. He had to hear a 'yes' from her, first.

"And this time, they demand I bring the Blue Slipper," Deborah's voice sobbed from nearby.

Startled, Nicholas propped himself on his elbow. He lay on the couch near the window. Deborah and Olivia stood only a few feet away near the press. Deborah, with tears streaking her cheeks and Olivia, with a letter in her hand. He joined them, at once.

"Lord Blair, whatever shall I do?" Deborah asked, twisting her fingers.

Silently, Olivia handed him the letter.

No more betrayals. This is not a game. Bring the two thousand pounds and the Blue Slipper to the 'An Enchanted Summer Evening' at the Theatre Royale. Leave them in the third-tier box during intermission. If they are not to be found, Lady Kendrick will receive the remaining pages of your letter, and right quick, that same night. This is not a game.

"The Theatre Royale?" Nicholas frowned.

"Right quick," Olivia murmured. "Mr. Pitt often uses that turn of phrase."

"Mr. Pitt?" Deborah breathed.

Nicholas shook his head. "The man is a fool, but fool enough for some act like this?" He paused. "Yet, only a fool would ask for the Blue Slipper. He will never be able to sell such a thing. The Blue Slipper is far too well known."

"Unless he broke it," Deborah choked. "Lady Kendrick. He's

going to give the letter to *Lady Kendrick*. Everyone in Glasgow will know my secret before the concert is over. Lord Deveraux..." She choked. "Oh, Olivia, he won't be able to wed me, not with the secret known."

"Then, we must be diligent," Nicholas said.

"Can we not confront the man?" Olivia mused. "Stll, that might only make him..."

At Deborah's fresh bout of sobs, she winced.

Nicholas nodded. Such a thought was better left unsaid. "I must see to Mr. Timms. The man may well have learned something from last night."

Olivia followed him to the door. "Can this be stopped?"

"Aye, lass." He took her hand gently between his. "We will find the man."

She nodded.

He kissed her hand then, not caring a whit about propriety, kissed her lips, so soft, so sweet.

"Later," he murmured in her ear, then left them.

He'd sent his coachman home the night before. It took longer than expected to wave a hired coach down, but soon, he was on his way to his hotel room.

Mr. Timms arrived, almost at once.

"'Tis strange, indeed, my lord." The man mopped his face. His waistcoat had popped another button. "My men and I never saw a thing. Whoever this is, they couldn't have seen us. I swear it."

"Then, why did they not arrive at the meeting place, and of more interest, how did they know Deborah stayed inside the townhouse? Were they watching her?" Nicholas paused by his room window and idly tapped on the sill.

"It might be of help to watch the lady," Mr. Timms suggested. "Perhaps them that are blackmailing her are closer than we think?"

Nicholas nodded. "Aye. Let's watch Mr. Pitt, as well."

"Aye, my lord. I'll not let whoever it is slip through my fingers a second time. Next time, we will catch him—or her. I swear it."

"Have your men watch after Deborah." Nicholas folded his arms.

"Aye, my lord. All things considering, perhaps we should watch after Miss Mackenzie, as well? You did mention she'd been robbed, and the letter was taken from her shop, was it not?"

"Indeed," Nicholas murmured. "Have your men follow her, as well."

"Aye, my lord. Night and day."

The days, most assuredly, but as for the nights? He would see to the nights himself.

CHAPTER 21

OLIVIA STOOD AT THE BACK OF THE OPERA HOUSE, AGAIN WIPING tears from her eyes. She could only laugh at herself. She'd heard Florinda sing the song countless times before, and looking at her now, singing on the stage, she couldn't help but feel a stab of jealousy, knowing Nicholas had kissed her—and more besides. Even so, the tears still flowed. The woman had the voice of an angel. Truly, there was no better singer to sing her father's songs.

As for Nicholas? Olivia smiled. In the past week and a half, he'd taught her the many delights of his tongue and the wonders of his fingers. There was no need for jealousy now, not when he spent his nights with *her*. Nae, tonight the world would hear her father's music. She'd sold every ticket. Florinda, the Lark of Paris, was the talk of Glasgow. Tonight, the mystery of her father's work would be unveiled. Olivia couldn't have wished for a more successful concert if she'd tried.

"Tonight," Mr. Pitt's voice huffed behind her.

She turned and forced back a grimace. Tonight, as well, they'd catch the blackmailer red-handed. She'd kept her eye on

Mr. Pitt the entire week, on the alert for any hint or sign of his guilt. She had seen nothing—not a single hint.

"Yes, Mr. Pitt," she replied. "Tonight. At long last."

"There won't be a dry eye in the house," the man puffed with pride, as if he were personally responsible for the entire venture.

"Indeed," Olivia murmured.

"Flowers, lad." Mr. Pitt turned away as a lanky, red-haired youth skipped down the stairs. "See that Mistress de Bussone's dressing room is filled with roses."

"Yes, sir."

"Move. Right quick."

Right quick. Olivia frowned. It was such an odd turn of phrase, and Mr. Pitt was the only man she'd ever heard use it. She watched him leave. Mr. Timms had searched the man's rooms in the theatre from top to bottom. He'd found no evidence of any kind, not one page of Deborah's letter. Guilt stabbed. If only she hadn't lost the blasted letter to begin with.

The church bells rang in the distance, interrupting her guilt. Excitement welled. It was time. Time now, to go home and ready herself. Time to slip into the dress Deborah had gifted her, and then to return, to see and hear the premiere of her father's music. Still, even now, she could scarcely believe the concert was, at last, happening.

Quickly, she hurried backstage and escaped the theatre to head across Glasgow Green. Above the trees, starlings swooped in ever-shifting clouds. Soon, night would fall, bringing with it the brilliance of the theatre chandeliers, the strains of the music, the applause.

Of course, her father wouldn't attend. He would be home, safe with his piano, with Mrs. Lambert by his side. She sighed. If only he could hear his music…but then, no doubt, he already heard symphonies in his heart.

"Miss Mackenzie."

Olivia paused at the edge of the park, recognizing Lord Randall's voice so very close behind. She hadn't seen him since the night of her grandfather's dinner party. Frankly, she hadn't spared him a thought. Slowly, she turned.

He stood behind her, elegantly dressed, his silver-handled walking stick looped over the crook of his arm. "Miss Mackenzie."

"Lord Randall," she acknowledged with a dip of her chin.

"It's so hard to reach you, with Lord Blair constantly hovering by your side." His eyes glittered with a coldness that sent a shiver down her spine—a very unpleasant one.

She frowned. "Why would you care to reach me?"

The man hesitated, then smiled. Something about the way his lips curved made her want to smack the smile straight off his face.

"Surely, you know that your grandfather has blessed a union between us," he said. "I beg your forgiveness in being so blunt, but I must—"

"Lord Randall, I am astounded. I have been clear with you from the start. I cannot be clearer. I will not wed you. *Ever.*"

Again, his face hardened, and again, she saw the flash of anger beneath his mask.

She made up her mind, at once. She wouldn't linger in the man's company a moment more. "Good day, my lord."

She hurried away, ignoring his calling of her name. He followed her for a time, but when she turned down her street, she spared a quick glance over her shoulder to see him no longer there. Relieved, she hurried into the shop.

"It is time, lass," Mrs. Lambert said, grinning widely.

"It is time," Olivia breathed in response.

THE DRESS FELT AS WONDERFUL CARESSING HER BODY AS IT looked in the mirror. The gold silk fell in soft folds, and the detailed stitching on the bodice glittered in the candlelight. Deborah had used gold thread. Olivia twirled in the mirror, feeling like a queen. Poor Deborah. If only she could enjoy this evening without the threat of blackmail hanging over her head —but then, with Lord Deveraux at her side, along with Mr. Timms and his men at the ready, perhaps soon, the blackmailer would be found.

She smoothed the skirt one last time, then hurried down the steps and into the parlor. At the door, she paused. The evening looked like so many others. Her father playing his piano, lost in his music, with Mrs. Lambert darning in her chair by the lamp.

"You look like a princess, lass," Mrs. Lambert grinned, her mole hairs dancing in agreement.

With a smile, Olivia glided to her father and planted a kiss on the top of his head. This night, he merely smiled absently in return and continued to play. It was just as well. Why disturb him?

"Lord Blair awaits you in the shop," Mrs. Lambert nodded toward the curtains.

His name made her pulse quicken, and with a quick nod of thanks, Olivia slipped from the parlor and into the shop. A single candle burned on the counter where Nicholas stood, dressed in black with a crisp white shirt, an elaborately tied gray cravat, and his black, silk-banded hat in his hands. The look in his eyes sent a tingle down the back of her neck.

"Come here, lass," he invited, his voice low.

He caught her fingers as she joined him and dropped a kiss on her knuckles before lifting his hand above her head to twirl her around.

"Hold still, my love," he whispered in her ear.

The coolness of a metal chain encircled her neck and she

glanced down. A diamond pendant lay against her collarbone. "What is this?" she gasped.

"A gift." He brushed his lips on the tender flesh beneath her ear. "Wed me."

Olivia shot him a scowl. "Must you tease me so? Be serious, if only for this night."

"I *am* serious."

"Come now, Lord Blair, you're a rake, and a man above my means." She crossed to the hook and removed her pelisse and hat. Truly, it was a shame to cover the splendor of her dress, but it couldn't be helped.

"Is this so wide a gulf you cannot cross?" he asked when she returned.

Olivia reached up and tweaked his nose. "Enough. No more foolishness." Then, her lightheartedness faded away. "The blackmailer—"

"Will be caught," he finished her sentence firmly.

She nodded.

"Then allow me?" He winged an arm.

He led her to his waiting carriage, but she was too excited to remember much of the drive. Everywhere she looked, gaily dressed men and women strolled toward the Theatre Royale. Before she knew it, Nicholas's carriage joined the line of those dropping patrons at the opera house's front entrance.

The Theatre Royale looked magnificent, living up to its name and more besides. Laughter and excitement filled the air. Women in their velvet, silk and satin evening gowns, with diamonds and other jewels glittering about their necks, milled about on the arms of elegantly clad men.

Olivia held her breath as Nicholas handed her down and escorted her to the top of the stairs. At the theatre door, she paused and looked behind her. Everywhere she turned, an array of color and lights met her eyes. It was an enchanted evening, indeed.

"Ah, Deborah," Nicholas murmured at her side.

Olivia turned to see the duke's carriage arrive at the bottom of the steps. The footman opened the door and Lord Deveraux emerged first to lift his hand and assist Deborah. She was beautiful, dressed in blue with sapphires glittering about her neck. The dark blue only served to accentuate her pale face, but as the future Duchess of Lennox, sapphires were a tradition she could not ignore.

Olivia held up her hand in greeting, then stopped in shock. Another man exited the carriage. The lamplight caught on the silver-streaked hair. Her grandfather. She watched him, unable to move.

"Do my eyes betray me?" Nicholas chuckled. "Is that truly the duke?"

His humorous words released her from her spell. "No doubt, he has come to judge me lacking," she said.

Nicholas merely laughed and patted her hand.

Deborah arrived, once again looking like a nervous bird. "You look beautiful, Olivia," she said.

"Thanks to you." Olivia squeezed her cousin's hands and added in a low voice, "Do not fret."

"I am trying," Deborah confessed with a nervous laugh. She lifted her reticule. "I have the package."

The package she was to leave in the opera box during intermission.

"It will all be over soon," Olivia promised.

The sounds of the musicians tuning their instruments rolled over the crowd.

"Come, my dear," Lord Deveraux held out his arm. "We must away to our seats."

"It is time," Nicholas said.

It was time. At so very long last. Strangely misty-eyed, Olivia allowed him to guide her forward, toward the stairs leading to their seats. From the corner of her eye, she spied Lord Randall approaching the stairs with Lady Kendrick on his arm. They were a strange couple, but she was glad to spare the man no further thought. She had far more pressing matters to attend.

It was slow going to their seats. It seemed as if every man and woman in Glasgow wished to speak with her in person, from offers of congratulations to inquires after her father's health. Over the heads of the crowd and on the stairs ahead of her, she spied the banker that had refused her funding. Catching her eye upon him, he paused and offered the deepest bow of respect.

Then, finally, Nicholas led her into the box. Deborah and Lord Deveraux had already taken their seats. Olivia had barely seated herself than the red velvet stage curtains began to open. A wave of applause circled the audience as Florinda stepped onto the stage to stand in a snow-white gown with three magnificent candelabras behind her.

She lifted one finger.

Silence fell. Utter. Complete.

Then, the first notes began to play.

Tears flooded Olivia's eyes. At last, her father's music played. She bowed her head and for a time, lost herself in her father's world.

The minutes passed, but Olivia scarcely noticed. The music flowed through her, pulling her back to her younger years, when her father worked the press and her mother tended their home. Laughter and love abounded. She could hear it all, in every note. She listened, caught up in a dream.

Then, the music ended.

The ushers brought candles into the audience below. Light filled the room. The audience clapped. Men and women shouted *brava, brava*, just as they had in her dream.

The bells announced the intermission.

Olivia drew a startled breath. How had time passed so quickly? She noticed Deborah fidgeting at her side.

"All will be well, Deborah," Olivia reassured as they exited the box.

"A message, for Lady Deborah," one of the ushers approached with a folded letter.

Deborah tensed. Lord Deveraux and Nicholas exchanged looks. With shaking hands, Deborah broke the seal.

"It's from him," she squeaked.

"What is it?" Nicholas demanded.

"I am to bring my reticule to the lobby," she whispered. "That is all."

"And?" Lord Deveraux prompted.

"He's to find me there."

"What the devil?" her fiancé spat.

"We will catch him," Nicholas assured. "I have more than one man lurking around Lady Kendrick. We'll be watchful of Mr. Pitt or any other who approaches her."

"Then, shall we?" Lord Deveraux stepped forward.

Deborah descended the stairs, clutching her reticule so tightly her knuckles had turned white. Olivia followed closely behind. Halfway down, she spied Mr. Pitt bobbing through the crowd, hurrying their way.

So, it *was* him.

Olivia glanced at Nicholas, but his gaze was locked on Mr. Pitt.

"Miss Mackenzie," Mr. Pitt called. "Miss Mackenzie." He pushed straight past Deborah and to herself. "You are wanted backstage," he said with a worried frown. "Is is a bit of a disaster, if I say so myself. Florinda's dressing room."

Olivia's eyes widened. "Disaster? Is she well? Can she still sing?" Of course, disaster would strike, and at the worst possible moment.

"Best run," the man hissed.

Again, ignoring Deborah, he hurried away. Olivia stared at his disappearing back. Was he not the blackmailer? He hadn't so much as spared Deborah a glance.

"It truly sounds important." Deborah sad. "You should go."

"How can I leave you?" Olivia gasped.

"I assure you, Deborah is safe in my care," Lord Deveraux insisted.

Olivia shot Nicholas a quizzical glance.

"Go." He lifted his brow at Mr. Pitt's disappearing, then returned his attention to her. "There's naught to fret over here. You are safe. Mr. Timms' men have you under their eye, I assure you."

She didn't have a choice. Truly. "I will hurry back," she promised.

She rushed away, ignoring the host of patrons calling out her name.

Mr. Pitt was nowhere to be found. She nearly ran back to Deborah, just to ensure her cousin's safety, but once she neared Florinda's dressing room, the unmistakable sound of angry voices sent her heart into a wild rhythm. She reached for the knob, but the door flew open beneath her touch. A woman stood, angry—nae, furious. Her hair loose and in disarray.

Olivia's mouth dropped open. "*Louisa.*"

Louisa Hamilton glared back at her, nostrils flaring, hands on her hips. "This, this strumpet *dares* to sing *my* songs?" Her voice rose in a crescendo. "This is *my* concert. *My* songs."

"Toss this *toad* to the street," Florinda spat from behind the mountain of roses filling the room.

Olivia blinked.

Some of the vases lay broken on the floor and the flowers crushed.

Louisa tossed her head and craned her neck over her shoulder. "Better a toad than a grunting pig—and with the looks of one, as well."

Candlelight caught the locket hanging about her neck.

Olivia's throat closed.

There was no mistaking it. Her mother's necklace.

With one swift jerk, she yanked the locket from Louisa's neck. "Where?" Olivia gasped. "Where did you get this?"

Louisa screeched. "Have you gone mad?" She waved a paper in front of Olivia's face. "This is *my* concert, and I have the contracts to *prove* it."

Olivia held still. The contracts. The stolen contracts. She snatched them from Louisa's hand. "Where did you get these?"

"Lord Randall gave them to me, and the necklace, as well," Louisa retorted in near hysteria. "He told me what you were up to. How you betrayed me…"

Olivia was no longer listening. The blood rushed to her ears. Lord Randall. Suddenly, the pieces fell into place. He'd paid for his music with the bent shilling. There weren't two, after all. As for the contracts and her mother's necklace, he must have broken into her house. Had he watched her that night through the window, when she'd taken the box out from beneath the floorboard? She shuddered. *He'd followed her home.*

The letter. *Deborah's letter.* He'd been there that day. Lord save her, he hadn't shown up at the cemetery the night of the dinner. He'd known Deborah hadn't left the house, *because he'd been there, standing amid the trees.* He'd clearly enjoyed torturing Deborah…and all the audacity he possessed, in asking her grandfather for her hand?

She shuddered. The blackmailer wasn't Mr. Pitt, at all. It was Lord Randall. No doubt, he'd written the letter in such a fashion to throw them off the scent.

With a gasp, she remembered. Lord save them all. Lady Kendrick. She'd seen him herself, escorting Lady Kendrick on his arm.

Olivia whirled and ran down the hall.

CHAPTER 22

NICHOLAS LEANED AGAINST THE RAILING AND WATCHED LADY Kendrick from under speculative brows. Lord Randall had arrived with her. He hovered at her side every instant, sitting by her, and now, offering her a glass of red wine. He'd played the attentive fool. A plethora of others had approached the woman, of course. After all, one would expect nothing less from Glasgow's premiere gossip. Still, while so many had exchanged words, nothing had changed hands.

Deborah made her way through the crowd, her reticule still clutched in her hand.

Nicholas straightened from the railing when Olivia arrived out of breath.

"Nicholas," she breathed, her green eyes wide. "It's Lord Randall."

"Randall?" he repeated.

"The blackmailer. It is Lord Randall."

The truth struck him, at once. Of course. Such a perfect fit for the man. Nicholas didn't hesitate. He took the stairs at a run. By the time he arrived at Lady Kendrick's side, Lord Randall had left her.

"Lord Nicholas," Lady Kendrick smiled.

Nicholas nodded and scanned the crowd. There. Near the balcony door.

He hurried after him and caught the man by the shoulder just as he stepped into the night air. Lord Randall whirled and swung his cane to strike, but years of brawling and dueling as a rake came to Nicholas's aid. He ducked and whirled, lifting his leg to execute a vicious kick. The cane flew from Lord Randall's grasp as he fell, sprawling backwards onto the balcony floor.

"Are you mad, Blair?" Lord Randall spat, attempting to rise.

Nicholas pinned him down with a booted foot to his throat. "You will pay for this."

"Pay?" Lord Randall hissed as best he could.

"You seek to blackmail your betters, do you?" Nicholas grated. He pressed his boot harder. "Where is the letter?"

"What letter?" Lord Randall breathed heavily.

"This letter," Olivia answered close behind.

Nicholas glanced sideways as she stepped into view, holding the silver handle of Lord Randall's cane in her hands. From it, a roll of paper half protruded.

"A hollow cane," Nicholas snorted. Of course. The man was a devious one, hiding the letter in plain sight.

Olivia glared. "You think to blackmail my cousin? You will pay, Lord Randall. No one interferes with Deborah's happiness. No one."

"She is ruined," Lord Randall seethed. "Soon enough—"

Nicholas silenced him with additional pressure to his foot. "What is this?"

Nicholas looked over just in time to witness the Duke of Lennox, plucking the letter from Olivia's hands.

"Nae." Olivia grabbed for it.

Her grandfather stopped her with a deadly look, then, Mr.

Timms and his men pushed their way through the crowd gathered at the balcony door.

"This is the man?" Mr. Timms blinked, surprised.

"Aye," Nicholas replied with a curt nod. "Take him away."

"Wait." The duke held up a hand.

Olivia made a strangled noise and again, reached for the letter, but it was too late. Clearly, the duke had seen enough.

Coldly, he approached Lord Randall. "Blackmail, is it?" Slowly, he knelt on one knee and whispered, "I will ruin you for this, Randall." He stood and faced Mr. Timms. "As Lord Blair says, take this bastard away."

Olivia closed her eyes. It was over. At last.

CHAPTER 23

NICHOLAS WATCHED OLIVIA WORK HER WAY THROUGH THE gathering. A week had passed since the concert. *An Enchanted Summer Evening* had been a smashing success. Glasgow still spoke of little else—barring the news of Lord Randall's fall from grace. True to his word, the duke had ruined the man.

Still, Olivia was primarily the talk of the town, and her father, as well. Every newspaper in Scotland and England carried the story of her father's music, sung by the famed Lark of Paris. The concert had exceeded even his highest hopes for her success. With a smile, he watched her circle the ballroom of the Duke of Lennox's country estate, Arbroath Hall. She moved with such poise, such grace, conversing easily with even the most cantankerous, manipulating them into smiles. By God, her talent was wasted building her music empire. She belonged in the government. He watched her from under hooded lids, his gaze snagging on the length of ribbon on her gown. Soon, he'd see her wearing such a ribbon, and nothing else.

"My dear son."

Nicholas cleared his throat and turned to see his mother bearing down upon him.

"I have been remiss in visiting," he acknowledged as she drew him into a warm embrace. "But I have been rather busy."

"No son should be so busy as to not visit his own mother— especially in the very same town," she chided, but then, he noticed the gleam in her eye. "At last, you are here at the very same time as my dearest friend's daughter. I have so wanted the two of you to meet."

Nicholas graced her with a smile. "Mother, I would be delighted to meet her, but I have made up my mind. I have decided to wed."

"Wed?" Her lips parted in surprise. "Surely, you jest?"

"I assure you, I do not."

"Who is she?"

"I shall bring her to you, shortly. At the moment, she is rather engaged." He angled his head toward Olivia, who spoke to Lord Deveraux near the punch table at the far end of the ballroom.

Lady Blair sighed. "I did so want you to meet Olivia."

Nicholas cocked a brow. "Olivia?"

"My dearest friend's daughter, Olivia Mackenzie," his mother replied. "Indeed, she is as a daughter to me."

Nicholas chuckled. His mother glanced at him in confusion, but he was prevented an explanation by the entrance of the Duke of Lennox, with Deborah on his arm. The voices in the room fell. Deborah moved to the center of the ballroom, dressed in sapphire blue with a matching string about her neck.

The Duke of Lennox clapped his hands. A footman appeared at the door, bearing a silver tray over his head upon which rested a small, wooden box. He stopped before the duke and bowed. Slowly, the duke opened the box and withdrew a small ceramic shoe, encrusted with sapphires. A chorus of 'ahhs' resounded through the chamber.

"Lords and Ladies," the duke raised his voice as he held the shoe aloft. "This day has been so very long in coming. I thank you, one and all, for your attendance on this joyous occasion: the announcement of my heir."

Applause circled the room.

Nicholas smiled at Olivia where she stood with Lord Deveraux. There had been rumors the duke was announcing Deborah's inheritance. Indeed, it was the only reason Olivia had agreed to attend. While her relations with her grandfather had improved since the concert, the progress could barely be measured. Still, he knew her to be secretly pleased the old man had attended.

"My granddaughter," the duke continued, "is a woman of rare constitution and strength, a fierce spirit who bows to none."

Nicholas arched a brow at Deborah. Surely, the duke jested.

"Loyal to her family, and of the utmost worth to carry forth the family name. Indeed, I could not ask for a fiercer protector of the line of Lennox," the duke continued, his voice growing hoarse with emotion. He lifted the sapphire shoe higher. "I am proud, Nae, both honored and humbled to announce the next Duchess of Lennox."

Again, the applause. Deborah was loyal enough, but it was the only word in the man's speech that applied. Oddly, Deborah was grinning widely, Nae, beaming from ear to ear as if she could barely hold her joy in check.

"Please," the duke continued when the applause abated. "Let me introduce you to Lady Olivia Mackenzie, my heir, the future Duchess of Lennox."

Nicholas froze.

Across the ballroom, he watched Olivia's face change from smiling widely at Deborah to utter confusion, and then, turn into one of utmost shock. Nicholas began to chuckle. Cheers mingled with the applause as the duke slowly approached her with Deborah practically skipping by his side. Of course, it all made sense now. Deborah had been in on the secret all along. The duke stopped before Olivia, almost appearing a bit wary— but then, with the history and nature of their relationship, Nicholas could hardly blame the man.

Silence fell.

Finally, Olivia's lips parted. "I do not understand."

The duke smiled. "I am correcting an error made long ago. I am bestowing upon you your mother's inheritance. One, so rightly earned."

Olivia swallowed, glanced around at the faces turned her way, then curtseyed. The duke's shoulders relaxed.

Once the applause had faded away and the music and merrymaking resumed, Nicholas threaded his way through the crowd to where Olivia stood by her grandfather's side, smiling graciously at the well-wishers lined up to greet her.

"I am expanding into London," he heard her say as he arrived.

"Aye," the duke grumbled, smiling his thanks at Lady Winthrop.

"And Paris," Olivia pressed before turning to greet Lord Bramwell and his wife. When they moved away, she turned back to the duke and added, "You might wish to reconsider this decision. "I will never stop publishing music."

The duke arched a brow. "No doubt, even the hounds of hell couldn't stop you. What chance have I?"

Olivia lifted her chin. "What of my father?"

The duke's head snapped around. Excusing himself from the crowd surrounding them, he turned to Deborah. "Show her."

Deborah grinned and held out a hand. "Come, Olivia." Catching sight of him, she added, "Nicholas, you come, too."

He followed, looping Olivia's arm through his as they left the ballroom. Somewhere, in the sea of faces, he spied his mother's astonished face. He flashed a grin in her general direction, then Deborah started up Arbroath Hall's grand staircase.

"I do not understand," Olivia said.

"I do," Deborah giggled. "I am so relieved, so happy. You will make such a wonderful Duchess. Clearly, you were born for it, dear cousin. So much more than I."

"But I cannot," Olivia replied. "I could never accept such a thing, not after the way he…"

"He seeks to set things right," Deborah assured as she led them down a corridor on the third floor.

"But my father…" Olivia began. Her voice trailed away as the strains of a piano drifted through a nearby door.

"Grandfather says to all that he is a most talented man." Deborah pointed to the last door at the end of the corridor. "He seems very happy, if I may say so."

Slowly, Olivia approached the door. Nicholas kept a step behind. The room was a spacious one, lined with windows to welcome the gentle evening light, and with the finest of pianos placed before the fireplace. On a rose brocade sofa several yards away, sat Mrs. Lambert, her knitting needles flashing in the lamplight.

Olivia stilled.

"Grandfather brought him here this very morning," Deborah explained in a hushed voice. "You will be living here now. That is, when you're not printing music. I heard grandfather saying how you will likely have a print house built nearby. He's even sent for several of London's finest printing presses as a gift."

Still, Olivia didn't move. With a smile, Deborah bobbed a curtsey and started toward the stairs and the gaiety of the ballroom below as Nicholas slipped up behind Olivia and wrapped his arms around her waist.

For a time, they stood, listening to her father play, but at the end of the third song, she suddenly twisted in his arms. He let her go. She passed down the hall, her fingers clenched, and then, at the sound of approaching voices, she reached for the nearest door and vanished inside.

He followed.

They stood in a bedroom, a small guest room, decorated in rose patterned paper with an ivy-green settee and four-poster bed.

"What is it, my love?" He came up behind her once again.

She faced him, tears rolling down her cheeks. "I...I have hated him for so long."

Nicholas smiled. "Your grandfather?"

She nodded.

"The two of you are so very much alike, my love." He chuckled.

Her brows furrowed with displeasure.

"Time." Nicholas ran his hands down her back. "Take time to learn who he is, my dear. He clearly is a man of regrets."

She nodded. The line of her brows deepened. "This is so... so unexpected."

"Aye." He dropped his voice. "Now, I fear, I cannot ask you to wed me any longer."

Olivia blinked. "I never took you seriously, Nicholas."

"You should have." He threaded his fingers through hers. "Now, it is too late. I can no longer ask. As a duchess, now, it is you who outranks *me*."

A light entered her eyes. Her lashes lowered. "Shall I ask you to wed me, Lord Blair?"

"I accept."

He kissed her, deeply, taking his time in tasting the sweetness of her mouth.

She tore her lips from his. "Take me," she whispered.

Take her. He would make her his. At last. How fortunate that they had picked a room with a bed. He caught her up in his arms and carried her to the bed, his cock hardening in anticipation as he lay back with her across the counterpane. As the ribbon about her waist fanned across the bed, he found himself grinning. With one swift jerk, he tore the ribbon free.

"Nicholas!" She stared at her ripped gown.

The tear revealed the curve of her breast. Blood rushed to his cock at the sight. He set the ribbon aside for later and slid his hand through the opening to cup her breast. She moaned and closed her eyes. He knew she'd like that. He caught her nipple between his fingers and teased it into a peak. He withdrew his hand, grabbed the material in each hand, and ripped her dress the rest of the way. Her eyes flew open in surprise.

"It's already ruined," he murmured lightly, quite enjoying himself and the sight of her breasts laid bare to his eyes.

Any further objection she might have had was shushed when he latched onto her breast and began to suck.

"Yes." She laced her fingers in his hair.

She was so responsive, so sensual. He swirled his tongue around her flesh and grazed her nipple with his teeth as he pulled the shreds of her gown and shift free from her winsome form.

Finally, she lay naked beneath him, just as he liked. He released her breast and began kissing his way down. She knew what he wanted. She opened her legs. Wide. He buried his face in her folds, tasting her dew on his tongue as he licked the line of her crease. Already, he was tugging at the buttons of his breeches.

"Yes, Nicholas." She arched her hips up to his tongue.

As the last button pulled free, he rose to his knees. She watched him shrug free of his shirt, then his breeches until, at last, he knelt beside her, as naked as she. Rising on an elbow, she reached for his cock. He inhaled sharply as she traced his length with a fingertip, up, then down, and then back up to outline the sensitive head.

When she, at last, collapsed back on the bed, he eyed her

with a wicked lift of his brow. Then, he slid his body over hers. Skin met skin. She was so soft. Like velvet. He kissed her, hard, as he slid a palm down her belly and slipped his finger between her folds. She was wet. Ready. But still, he didn't want to take her, not yet. Sucking her bottom lip, he slowly let it go and reached for the ribbon.

"What are you doing?" Her eyes locked onto the length of satin.

He took his time tying the ribbon about her waist. He suckled each breast and played with her folds more than once before finally, he'd fastened the satin about her waist and looped the long ends around her back to draw them up between her folds. The sight of the ribbon encompassing her body was even more erotic than he had imagined. His cock lengthened. It was torture, an exquisite one, viewing her pink folds wrapped in ribbon.

Finally, he could no longer resist. Sliding the ribbon aside, he aligned his shaft with her entrance and slowly pushed forward. The sight of her body accepting him, inch by inch, only fueled his passion. By God, he felt harder than marble. He thrust his hips forward, pushing deeper until he felt her maidenhead resist him.

He paused. "This will hurt, my love."

"Quickly," she panted. "Take me, quickly."

She'd scarcely said the words before he granted her wish. In a single stroke, he was through. She gasped, rising up, but he caught her in a kiss. Almost at once, she began to buck, signaling her pain had already eased. He met her eagerly.

She was so sensual, such a wildly passionate creature, so perfect a match. They moved together, with an ever-increasing vigor. She was sweet blessed heaven, taking him completely, her flesh molding around his. He felt his seed rise.

He couldn't finish before her. Desperately, he held onto every shred of control. His breath turned ragged. He knew she was close. He'd watched her release enough times over the past few weeks to recognize the signs. She closed her eyes, moving freely, uninhibited by her passion. She began to shudder. He thrust harder. With a gasped, he released his seed, as she bucked in the throes of her release.

Finally, when the last waves of their passion faded, he slid his body off hers and lay by her side. "My love, will you marry me?"

She opened her eyes, slowly. "Is this a jest?"

"Nae," he whispered. "It never was. Not once."

Her eyes widened, then, she said the words he so longed to hear, "Yes, my love."

EPILOGUE

A Year Later

"I understand, Olivia," the Duke of Lennox said as he prepared to enter his carriage.

"They will try every trick, grandfather," Olivia advised.

The old man's eyes gleamed, as they ever did whenever she called him that. Nicholas suppressed a smile. Now that he knew the man better, it was clear from the start that his gruffness had always been more a show than genuine.

"Don't settle for more than the agreed upon sum," she continued as the carriage door snapped shut behind him.

"I will pay less," he replied testily before drawing the curtains across the window with a jerk of his wrist.

Olivia grinned as the carriage lurched away. "He will," she said with a note of pride. "He's the best negotiator I could ask for."

"Well, you will need him," Nicholas said with a yawn. "Now that you are opening your second publishing house in London."

"True." Olivia nodded absently.

Nicholas guided her from the carriage drive to the gardens behind his mother's house. The past year had rendered Olivia a wealthy woman. Her reputation as a music publisher and a woman with a fine ear for talent had spread beyond Scotland and England to the continent.

"We should visit France," Olivia murmured. "No doubt, the venues to—"

"Hush," Nicholas interrupted.

She blinked and glanced up at him. "Why?"

He grinned. "Do you not know where you are, my love?"

She glanced around, and then understanding dawned in her eyes. "The hedgerow."

"Where we first met," he teased. "The kiss that changed my life."

"And mine," she was quick to say.

Then, she stepped up to him and ran her palms over his chest. The minx. She knew exactly what her touch did to him.

"Kiss me." She peered up at him through half-lowered lashes. "Kiss me, again."

"I will not stop at a kiss. Did I not tell you from the start? When a man sees something he wants, he goes after it."

Olivia laughed. "No more than a woman." She slipped her hand into his breeches.

He moaned with pleasure as her fingers closed around his shaft.

Aye, they were the perfect match.

SNEAK PEEK AT A STRANGER'S PROMISE

LORDS OF CHANCE BOOK ONE

TARAH SCOTT

Penniless and jilted, Charlotte Atchenson accepts a position as governess to Lord Alistair Cassilis 's illegitimate children. When Eliza sets foot in the Scottish lord's carriage, she faces the most dangerous foe a woman can face: a charming rogue. The danger is not only to her heart, however, but to her life, as well.

In an effort to deny her son's illegitimate children, Alistair's stepmother insists on a dour governess who will break their rebellious spirits. Alistair, however, decides that the pretty lass with a colorful French vocabulary who shows up in his step-mother's drawing room is exactly what the children need. If the notion offends his stepmother, all the better. If the lass is what he needs...well, a man can't ask for more. His stepmother doesn't intend for Alistair to open his heart to her grandchildren, or the woman who cares for them. Her plans include forcing them onto the streets.

CHAPTER 1

London, February 1814

"Scandalous." Captain Edwards sniffed in disdain. Charlotte tried not to wince when he turned his icy gaze from the store window to her. "No wife of mine would even *look* at such a gown." His bearded jaw clenched, he added in an even stronger censorious tone, "Frankly, Charlotte, I am disappointed."

We aren't married—yet, Charlotte retorted in her mind, and caught herself mid-roll of her eyes.

She pushed her prim straw bonnet back from her face and turned back to the shop window for another look. The gown floated there like a dream come true. Cut in the latest fashion and trimmed with embroidered rosebuds, lace, and tiny seed pearls, its sweeping, crimson silk skirt fell in a tumble of soft, sensuous folds. The dressmaker had even angled several mirrors around the masterpiece to highlight the different views.

Charlotte grinned. If she squinted her eyes and tilted her

head just a little to the left, she could almost imagine herself wearing the confection. In her mind's eye, an obliging shaft of winter sunlight caught the playful spark in her eyes along with the brilliant gold of her unruly brown curls, a contrast against the cream taffeta as she whirled in the dress.

Her future husband's heavy hand fell upon her shoulder. She jarred back into the moment and caught his reflection in the window. A toned and muscular tower of a man, resplendent in a Queen's fine scarlet coat with its gold braid and polished brass buttons. A gallantly handsome figure, to be sure —at first glance, anyway. A deeper inspection revealed chilling blue eyes and the vein on his forehead pulsed in disapproval, a vein that betrayed an ever-present simmering rage.

"I insist we leave, Charlotte." He grasped her arm. "A virtuous woman would never soil her father's good name—nor *mine*—by wearing such an abomination."

Charlotte suppressed a snort. "I merely thought it pretty, Captain Edwards."

"As my future wife, I insist you think no such thing." He looped his arm through hers and pulled her away from the shop window.

This time, she did roll her eyes. Heavens, did the man seek to control her thoughts? She snorted.

Captain Edwards paused midstride and peered down at her through narrowed eyes. "Are you mocking me?"

Charlotte thinned her lips in a grim line. She'd witnessed the Captain's temper often enough to regret her acceptance of his marriage proposal—a proposal her father had pressured her to accept at the tender age of sixteen. Her father, a major in the Queen's army, found Captain Edwards quite the catch. Not only was he a decorated captain, but a distant cousin to a baronet. Later, she learned her father owed the man a great deal of money. The discovery gave her courage. She'd begged her father to allow her to end the engagement, but he thought it far too late, and reminded her that he valued loyalty and faithfulness above all else—after the balance of his bank account, of course.

Still, she tried to change his mind, but whenever she broached the matter, he invariably replied, "It is *you* who must change, Charlotte. You are proud and willful. Be grateful the man still wants you. Heed his guidance. Marriage isn't pleasure. Marriage is work. When you're older, you'll understand. Now, *enough* of this foolishness."

Well, now she was older and she understood very well. Her father sought only to protect his own interests—not hers.

"*I am speaking to you, Charlotte.*" Captain Edwards gave her arm a rough shake. "I repeat, are you mocking me?"

Charlotte blinked. She cleared her throat, then answered in the most placating of tones, "No, sir."

He searched her face, clearly—and rightly—suspicious of her sincerity before nodding in satisfaction. Anchoring her arm tightly under his, he resumed their walk down the icy, snow-covered street.

"I know you think me harsh, Charlotte," he said. "But I've only your best interests at heart. Be grateful I am here to guide you. Because of me, you have blossomed into a virtuous woman, a woman worthy of becoming my wife. You've changed so much from when I met you as an undisciplined young girl of fifteen."

Charlotte looked away, in an effort to keep her anger in check. If only she *hadn't* met him that summer six years ago, that dreadful day when he'd first stepped foot in her father's home. She'd been far too young and impressionable to see what he truly was: an insufferable, judgmental boor of a prig—and a prig with a raging temper at that.

"Now, you are of an age where one expects you to have overcome your flaws," he droned on, puffing his chest pompously with each judging word. "The unhappy catastrophe of your mother's death as a child resulted in your lack of a proper upbringing, but…"

Charlotte let his voice fade into the background and took a deep lungful of the crisp, clean winter air. She'd heard this speech countless times. Her mother had died in childbirth, leaving her newborn daughter with only a name and a leather-bound cookery book. And with her father stationed in far-off India, Charlotte and cookbook passed between various family members for a time. She'd finally found a happy home with an elderly, distant relative, a retired Navy man who taught her Greek philosophy and the fine art of swearing. She'd been delightfully happy. Then he passed away and shortly after, her father returned from abroad.

"A humble, subservient wife, Charlotte," the pompous man at her side continued. "One who wears only *modest* attire. You must be the very model of propriety…"

A dark cloud passed over the sun. Stifling a yawn, Charlotte stared at the sudden snowflakes swirling down from above and tracked their descent from the sky as they flurried around the streetlamps along the lane. If only she could be as free to simply float away.

"Respect, duty, and honor," Captain Edwards kept on. "Discipline and fortitude. A woman to remain by my side through life's fortunes and misfortunes. Do you not agree that these are the obligations of a proper wife, Charlotte?"

"Yes, sir," she mumbled dutifully.

A break in the buildings ahead offered a sudden tantalizing glimpse of the Frost Fair spread out on the frozen Thames below. She'd read about it in the papers, but in person, it was fabulous, a living painting of women in brightly beribboned, feathered bonnets, men in velvet top hats, and children skating on the ice, toffee apples in hand. Painters lined the river banks, squinted in the darkening afternoon with brushes in hand as they captured the gaiety of the wondrous occasion on their canvases. Men on stilts threaded through the crowds gathered to watch the puppet shows and gape at the elephant by Black Friar's Bridge, used periodically to test the strength of the ice.

Suddenly, Captain Edwards cupped her chin and forced her eyes up to his. "What do you say to that?" he asked in a deep voice.

Charlotte blinked, startled by the unexpectedness of his move. He usually railed on for a good half hour or so. She twisted her lips and tried in vain to recall his words. "*Da*—uh… dare I agree, sir?" She caught herself at the last second and swiftly changed *damnation* into *dare*.

His blue eyes remained aloof, cool, and critical. She bit her lip, in hopes her reply a sufficient one to whatever he'd asked.

His lips spread into a slow smile. "I am pleased, Charlotte."

She let out a breath of relief.

"Then we agree," he said. "We will wed this summer. At last."

Charlotte choked. *This summer?*

"Charlotte!" a woman's frantic voice called from behind. "*Charlotte!*"

Charlotte whirled. The butcher's wife waved her apron as she ran toward them, sliding in the icy snow.

"Go home, girl, home. At once," the woman wheezed as she arrived. "It's Major Atchenson, your father. There's been an accident."

An accident. Two simple words that changed Charlotte's life forever.

Alone in the empty London townhouse, Charlotte huddled next to the kitchen stove in a solemn mood, as howling winds brought more snow. The coal hadn't lasted more than a week after her father's death. Unable to afford more, she'd resorted to what wood she could find, but with harsh winter weather, everyone in London searched as well, and she found precious little. She'd been reduced to buying twisted sticks of soiled straw from the hotel stables at the end of the lane, but it flamed so fast it provided little heat.

Now, she stared at the stove, wondering what she had left to burn. The creditors had taken everything.

Well…she had her relatives' letters.

With a bitter, mirthless smile, she tossed them into the stove, lit the match, then watched the heartless missives catch fire, all of them variations of the same *we cannot provide any assistance...* Cannot or will not? It didn't matter. She'd find her own way.

Shawl drawn tight around her shoulders, Charlotte remained seated before the stove long after the last letter curled into ash. She now understood the meaning of 'nightmare.' She'd been living in one the past few weeks.

"An accident," the constable had called her father's death. He'd fallen through the ice and drowned in the Thames. She hadn't believed them. She still didn't. Not after seeing the elephant standing on the river ice that very same day. How could her father break ice that could withstand the weight of an elephant? The idea stretched the imagination beyond credibility, but what could she do? No one cared—even *before* the creditors descended upon her like wild dogs.

Tears wet her lashes. She'd returned from the churchyard, having just seen her father buried, to find the creditors hovering like vultures at the townhouse's front door.

"What is this?" Captain Edwards had stepped to the forefront of the funeral party to confront the men. "What business have you here?"

They'd answered that their business concerned promissory notes long past due and letters from banks with demands for immediate compensation to the sum of several thousand pounds. At that, every head in the funeral party had turned.

Tongues tutted. Captain Edwards' mouth had dropped open in shock.

"Gaming debts," someone said.

"A swindler," said another.

"Scandal," they all agreed.

The creditors took everything. Even her mother's leather-bound cookery book.

Charlotte couldn't recall much after that, except for the beauty of the snowflakes swirling down from the sky to gently kiss her tear-stained cheeks.

The ring of St. Clement's bells in the distance jolted her back to the present.

"You weep more for the cookery book than your fiancé, Charlotte." She laughed bitterly and drew in a long, shaky breath.

Just an hour ago, Captain Edwards stood in the kitchen and commented on the lack of coal. He then handed her the last letter, saying, "As you know, Miss Atchenson, a man of my position must choose his wife with care, a woman from an upstanding family. I have done all I can for you."

Charlotte had stared in surprise. Yes, he'd stood by her side as they'd lowered her father into his grave, but so had many others. He'd done precious little else—ah, besides deliver the letter.

"I shall not marry you. I cannot besmirch my good name," he'd continued, pompous to the end. "Your father…well, the evidence of his scandalous behavior is undeniable." She stood frozen as he pulled a small leather bag from his waistcoat and tossed it at her feet. "This is my final act of kindness. Ten shillings."

Ten? Ten shillings? Fury swept through her anew at the memory of how she'd grabbed the bag from the floor, slapped it hard against his chest, and shouted, "What use have I for ten shillings when I have more than a thousand demands for the paltry sum?" She hadn't stopped there. She'd said the words she'd longed to say for years, "You are an arrogant ass, a fool and a bully. How thankful I am to not wed such a cruel, heartless and hypocritical man. Not even a month ago, did you not speak to me of respect, duty, and honor? Discipline? Of standing by your side through all the trials of life's fortunes and misfortunes? Or is it only the woman who must remain faithful?"

A dark color had stained his cheeks and he'd raised his hand. She took a faltering step back, then caught herself.

They stared at one another for several long moments before his hand slowly dropped. "Do not seek me out, Charlotte. I shall no longer acknowledge you." Then he left, his pittance clutched in his hand.

Charlotte smiled at the ashes inside the stove. Despite her destitute circumstances, she couldn't deny the sense of freedom, the weight that had been lifted from her shoulders. "You should've taken the coins, Charlotte," she criticized with a rueful shake of her head. "Ten shillings are better than none when you've eaten the last of the salted haddock and every doorstep you've stood on has turned you away."

She'd been unable to find work, even as a scullery maid.

With a sigh, she rose and stalked to the empty parlor with its undressed windows, for the creditors had taken even the worn damask curtains. She leaned her forehead against the frozen windowpane and looked out at the winter stillness blanketing the city. Only the streetlamps shone like beacons in the night.

"Tomorrow." She clenched her hands in determination. "Tomorrow this nightmare will end."

Tomorrow she would find employment. She had to. If she didn't, she'd be forced out onto London's frozen streets or into debtor's prison in less than a week, since her father still owed more than what his life had been worth.

CHAPTER 2

ALISTAIR JAMES, BARON AISLA, 11TH EARL OF CASSILIS, AND Laird of Castle Culzean, made quite the formidable picture standing before the fireplace in his aunt's Mayfair townhouse parlor. Dressed in a stylish, dark blue waistcoat with a silk cravat tied in the latest fashion, the handsome Scottish lord loomed tall, broad-shouldered, and muscular in an elegantly lean way. His bright green eyes and dimpled chin, combined with the sensual curl of his lip, made him the talk of the town— particularly since he rarely graced it with his presence. His aunt had spent the last ten minutes harping on this very subject instead of discussing the real matter at hand.

"And shall we now discuss the governesses you have chosen?" he at last interjected. "On my honor, I will no' have a one of them." Alistair pressed his mouth into a firm line of disapproval. He raised an elegant hand to cut his aunt's diatribe short. "Hags. The lot of them."

Lady Prescott's eyes popped in surprise. "Hags?" she gasped. "The last *two* governesses brought impeccable letters of recommendation, Alistair. Lady *Boswell's* recommendations, no less."

Alistair let the mocking arch of his brow express his

opinion of Lady Boswell, by far the cruelest gossipmonger in the *ton*—after his aunt, of course. He eyed the woman as she sat on her gilded, brocade chair like a queen on her throne, her aged face a mask of dissatisfaction and her mouth set in a permanent, judgmental frown. He held nothing in common with her—or any of his father's kin, for that matter.

"Frankly, why do you bother?" His aunt waved her Spanish, black-lace fan. "The children are…" Her voice trailed away and her nostrils flared again, this time in distaste.

Alistair pinned her with a stare. "The children are?" he prompted.

Lady Prescott knew better than to answer. "I would think *you* would understand," she huffed instead and, unable to bear his stern gaze, glanced away.

"Oh, I understand," he replied in a lethally soft voice. "I truly do."

The old woman stiffened. "Your situation was entirely different from theirs. Your mother was…was…well, your father wed her, did he not? In the end? Even though she was nothing but a scullery maid."

Nothing but a scullery maid. How many times had he felt the stinging slap of those words? Yes, in the end, his father *had* set things right, but the final act of legitimizing his estranged, eldest son hadn't stemmed from honor or remorse. His father simply had no choice—not if he wished his legacy to survive. Obsessed with rebuilding Castle Culzean at the expense of all else, the old earl had bankrupted his entire estate. It was either recognize Alistair—and the vast fortune he'd accumulated in his own right, a fortune that could pay the bills—or see the castle and his legacy sold off to the highest bidder.

The sudden discovery of his parents' wedding certificate after so many years smacked of deceit, but no one contested the matter in court. Why should they? They needed Alistair to set the estate to rights if they wanted their yearly sums. Oh, his stepmother had been furious, but her son, Charles, had seemed only relieved. He'd promptly moved to London to carouse and hop from one scandal to another, which meant Alistair himself had to travel down from the north to mop up the mess.

Lady Prescott rapped her fan on the arm of her chair to capture his attention. He lifted a brow in question.

"As I was *saying*, Alistair," she repeated, her lips puckered in the displeasure of finding herself ignored. "The children could belong to *anyone*. How can we be certain Charles even fathered the brats?"

Alistair expelled an exasperated breath. "Take a wee look at their eyes," he grated. "Even *you* cannot deny the Cassilis green." Both children shared the bright, distinct Cassilis green with flecks of blue around the pupils surrounded by a darker rich, deep emerald ring.

Lady Prescott's double chin jiggled in distaste. "Well, the woman was a…" She paused to grimace behind her fan.

"A mere laundress?" Alistair finished for her.

"Yes, I will say it, Alistair. The woman was a low-born laundress." The words burst from her mouth as if she could not hold them back. "Let *her* relations take the mongrel, beggar children in. It's unfitting we should be involved. Our reputation! Charles is a high-born—"

"Drunken sot," Alistair inserted coolly. "A sot refusing to provide for his offspring, and a sot happy to abandon them upon your doorstep so he may carouse on the continent. Good God, woman, can you truly suggest we abandon two wee, motherless children on the streets? Simply because their mother was—heaven forbid—a mere *laundress?*"

His aunt bristled like a hedgehog, her lips pressed so tightly together they turned white. "Alistair, your reputation—"

"Reputation?" he interrupted with a dry chuckle. "I should think my reputation would suffer should I *not* accept responsibility for the poor, motherless children." He held his hands up again, cutting her off. "My decision is made. The lad and lassie travel with me to Culzean, and that's the end of the matter."

Lady Prescott fluttered her fan again, affecting an injured air. "Very well, take them, if you insist, but they hardly need a governess. Let them learn a trade. They're well-born beggars at best and, as such, beneath the notice of polite society."

Alistair lifted his brow a contemptuous notch higher, astonished at the woman's audacity. "I am curious," he murmured. "Those many years ago, after my mother died and I found myself on my father's doorstep...whose idea was it then, to send me to the stables?" He'd arrived at his father's castle, a lad of eight—and had been promptly put to work mucking the stables.

Lady Prescott gave her fan a vicious snap. "We had to protect your father's reputation," she answered through tight lips. "You've no cause to be ungrateful. You're the earl now, aren't you? And this many years later, I am *still* providing assistance. I found eight highly *respected* governesses to care for the two children, Alistair. Eight. Yet, you have refused them all. What am I to do?"

So, if she hadn't sent him to the stables, she'd definitely participated in the notion. He shook his head. Just how hard and withered was her old heart?

"Eight, I repeat." She fanned her cheeks. "Eight."

Alistair folded his arms. Aye, she'd found eight governesses. Eight highly *prejudiced* old biddies who'd fluttered horrified eyelashes upon discovering they'd be educating two children of dubious parentage in a remote Scottish castle near the sea. He'd suffered enough in his youth with such women. He wasn't about to inflict the same kind of pain on two motherless bairns.

A knock on the parlor door prohibited further conversation, and a mob-capped maid entered to whisper hurriedly in his aunt's ear.

"Absolutely *horrifying*," Lady Prescott tutted behind her ever-present fan. "And she is on my *front* doorstep? Whatever is the world coming to? Are you certain I know a Major Atchenson? Why would his daughter come here?"

Alistair tilted his head, curious.

"Yes, my lady." The maid bobbed a curtsey. "Major Atchenson saved your son, young master George, in the war."

Lady Prescott's eyes widened. "Heavens! The very same Major Atchenson? How can that be? Such an ignoble end..." Her fan fluttered furiously. "No, no, I cannot...the gossip alone...no, I can't have her in my household. Show her in, but interrupt me in two minutes, two minutes, mind you. Claim an urgent matter begs my attention and send her away. I'll make certain she doesn't return."

Alistair stared, speechless. Had the woman no shame?

The maid left, then returned with a young woman dressed in a modest, brown, quilted Spencer jacket over a simple high-waist, blue gown, and a straw bonnet in hand.

Alistair's breath caught. She stood just inside the door, a perfect example of feminine beauty, a delicate and pale tragic angel. Her dark-lashed hazel eyes held deep-seated pain and her full downturned lips, betrayed a healthy sense of unease. She'd twisted her gold-tinted, brown locks into a simple bun, but several rebellious strands had escaped and curled around her neck. He dropped his gaze over the soft curve of her jaw.

"Miss Atchenson," his aunt raised her voice in greeting. "Allow me to offer you my sympathies, child. Such a shock, such a shock." She smiled, a most disingenuous smile.

Miss Atchenson dipped into a respectful curtsey to his aunt, then darted an uncertain glance at him. Alistair nodded a polite reply.

Lady Prescott tilted her head his way. "My nephew, Lord Alistair James, Baron Aisla and 11th Earl of Cassilis."

Alistair leveled Lady Cassilis a thin-lipped look. Could her boastful tone possibly be in poorer taste?

"I am told you're seeking *employment*, Miss Atchenson," his aunt addressed the young woman again. The lass brightened and opened her mouth to respond, but the old woman barreled on, "Considering your unfortunate circumstances, I would think it wise for you to look in the country. Perhaps Ireland?"

Miss Atchenson caught her breath. "I...see, my lady."

The maid rushed into the room. "Lady Prescott, a most urgent matter requires your immediate attention."

Alistair folded his arms across his chest. "One urgent matter," he said with a sardonic twist of his lips. "As ordered."

The women in the room froze.

He stepped forward and bowed. "Miss Atchenson, allow me to assist you whilst my dearest aunt of aunts deals with her urgent matter. Our family stands indebted to yours. Without your father's courageous action, my cousin George would no longer grace his mother's dinner table. Is that not true, Lady Prescott?"

His aunt recovered first. With an angry snap of her fan, she scowled at the maid. "The matter will have to wait. I must handle Miss Atchenson's predicament first." She turned to Alistair and added, "My dear boy, pray do not involve yourself. These things are far beneath your attention."

From the expression on her face, it was clear she thought him anything *but* 'dear.' He smiled, a cool, warning smile, and faced the young woman. Miss Atchenson regarded him uneasily. Another victim of the *ton*, to be sure. Well, now that he held a position of some authority, he knew by far the easiest way to provide true assistance to the lass was to face the gossip and rumors head-on.

"Forgive my frankness, Miss Atchenson," he addressed her as kindly as he could, "but might I inquire as to the nature of these 'unfortunate circumstances' my aunt has mentioned?"

Her eyes widened in surprise.

Lady Prescott gasped, horrified. "Heavens, Alistair, how unseemly."

"I mean no disrespect." He summoned a smile. "How can I help otherwise, pray tell?"

Miss Atchenson bravely smiled back. "My father recently met an unexpected and disgraceful end, my lord." Her voice, strong and low, held a musical quality.

For all of her talk of his approach being unseemly, his aunt had no problems jumping in. "Quite shocking." Her eyes lit with the thrill of gossip. "It was in every paper, Alistair, the week before you arrived. *Every* paper. Gambling debts and mismanagement of funds. Thousands of pounds. A decorated major! Such a disgrace. And now? The drinking. There's even talk of frequent visits to houses of ill repute. Why, Lady Witherby says his death was rather too convenient to be an accident and that he, well, you know…" She let her voice trail suggestively away.

Miss Atchenson's eyes flashed, but her lips remained firmly sealed. Aye, the lass obviously wished to defend her father. He found her response and restraint admirable.

Alistair lifted a brow at his aunt's haughty conceit, and couldn't resist saying, "What was that, Lady Prescott? Mismanagement of funds, you say? Rather reminds one of Castle Culzean's former laird, does it not?"

Lady Prescott's jaw dropped open. "Your father had *nothing* in common with—"

"He spent thousands of pounds he did not have," he cut her short. As she sucked in a shocked breath and furiously fanned her reddened cheeks, he eyed the young woman once again. "And what position…" he began, then, a sudden idea crossed his mind. "I assume you read and write, Miss Atchenson?"

His aunt's fan abruptly stilled.

Miss Atchenson's gaze darted quickly between them. "Yes,

my lord."

"You hold some basic knowledge of deportment and polite society? A smattering of French? Can you play at least one song on the pianoforte?"

She hesitated, then nodded.

"Absolutely *not*, Alistair." Lady Prescott pushed to her feet. "You preside over an ancient and noble Scottish house. *Think of your reputation, young sir.*"

Reputation. She couldn't have picked a better word to egg him on. "I need a governess to oversee two wee children at Castle Culzean, clan Cassilis's ancestral home on the Ayrshire coast," he continued smoothly. "A lad and a lassie, raised in London by their mother, a recently deceased laundress and, until now, without proper knowledge of their father's station in life. Were you to secure this position, you would teach them their letters and the ways of polite Society." At this point, the other governesses had flinched. He paused and studied the young woman's reaction.

Miss Atchenson hesitated, then dropped another nervous curtsey. "I am most honored for your consideration, my lord, but I am more suited to the scullery."

Scullery? The word tugged at his heart, reminding him of his mother. "Why not a governess?" he pressed.

She took a deep breath and answered with candor, "I know nothing of raising genteel children, my lord."

Genteel children. His lip curled in a smile. "Aye, you will do quite nicely, Miss Atchenson. The position is yours. I grow weary of London. We leave for Castle Culzean at once. I will send a man with you to gather your things."

Miss Atchenson's eyes widened.

"Have you gone mad?" Lady Prescott struggled to catch her breath.

He eyed the young woman before him. Had he? He didn't really know, but for some odd reason, he didn't truly care.

CPSIA information can be obtained
at www.ICGtesting.com
Printed in the USA
BVHW040031091222
653825BV00003B/19